Henry Ingersoll Bowditch

Nat the Navigator

Henry Ingersoll Bowditch

Nat the Navigator

ISBN/EAN: 9783337333591

Printed in Europe, USA, Canada, Australia, Japan

Cover: Foto ©Andreas Hilbeck / pixelio.de

More available books at **www.hansebooks.com**

A LIFE

OF

NATHANIEL BOWDITCH.

FOR YOUNG PERSONS.

The House in which he lived when a little Child.

BOSTON:
LEE AND SHEPARD.
1870.

MOVED by feelings I could scarcely comprehend, while, at the same time, they were most sweet to me, I was led to talk with the pupils of the Warren Street Chapel on the Sunday afternoon after my father died. The subjects were his active and good life and happy death. I am aware that some of my nearest friends thought it strange that my heart, on the occasion of his death, was filled with a kind of joy rather than with sadness. To them I could merely say, that an event so calm, and under such circumstances of suffering as he then was, suggested to me nothing like real sorrow. I wished my young companions to feel as I did, and that, in their minds, a quiet death following a good life should be clothed with beauty, and that they might thus be led to believe that, in accordance with the Scotch proverb, "A gude life makes a gude end. At least it helps weel." Horace Mann was present during the address. Being deeply interested in the education of the young, he requested me to prepare for his Common School Journal a sketch similar to that I had spoken. In accordance with that desire, a memoir was prepared, and after its publication the Warren Street Chapel Association requested that it should be put, with some revision, into this form. And as it was originally prepared for, and dedicated to, the pupils of that institution,

SO I NOW DEDICATE IT

ANEW TO THE

GIRLS AND BOYS OF WARREN STREET CHAPEL.

CONTENTS.

CHAPTER I.

From 1773 to 1784 — under 10 years of age.

CHAPTER II.

From 1784 to 1795 — between the ages of 10 and 21.

CHAPTER III.

From 1784 to 1796 — age, 10–22.

Apprenticeship continued. — Favorite of his companions. — Learns music; neglects his studies for a

CHAPTER IV.

From 1796 to 1797 — age, 23-4.

CHAPTER V.

From 1797 to 1800 — age, 24-7.

CHAPTER VI.

From 1800 *to* 1803 — *age,* 27-30.

CHAPTER VII.

CHAPTER VIII.

From 1803 *to* 1817 — *age,* 30-44.

CHAPTER IX.

From 1803 *to* 1823 — *age*, 30–50.

CHAPTER X.

CHAPTER XI.

CHAPTER XII.

Death, March 17, 1838, aged 65.

NAT THE NAVIGATOR.

CHAPTER I.

From 1773 to 1784 — under 10 years of age.

Birth. — Childhood.

NATHANIEL BOWDITCH, whose history I shall relate to you, was one whose character and actions presented many circumstances which cannot fail of being interesting to you. He died more than thirty years ago, in Boston; and, from having been a poor and ignorant boy, he became a man known all over the world for his great learning, while at the same time he was beloved for the goodness of his heart and the integrity of his character. May the perusal of his history excite some of you to imitate his virtues and his energy.

He was born in Salem, a town about fourteen miles from Boston, the capital city of our State of Massachusetts. His birthday was March 26, 1773. His father was at first a cooper, and afterwards a shipmaster. He and his wife were exceedingly poor, and they had many children. Nat was the fourth child. He had two sisters and three brothers. When he was about two and a half years old, his parents removed to a very small wooden house in Danvers, about three miles from Salem; and here the boy attended school for the first time, and began to show those generous feelings, and that love of learning, which he displayed so much in after-life. A few years ago the old school-house in which he learned to spell and read remained entire. It was an old-fashioned building, with a long, slanting roof, which, at the back of the house, nearly reached the ground. Its single chimney, with many curious and pretty corners, then rose in the middle of the roof, as it had for ninety years. Around the dwelling is a grass plat, upon which he used, when a

HIS FIRST SCHOOL-HOUSE.

child like yourselves, to play with his schoolmates. It was planted with shrubs, such as
the farmers most need. The house in which
he lived still stands nearly opposite that in
which the school was kept. This house formerly had but two rooms in it, and all its
furniture was of the simplest kind.

I visited the relations of the schoolmistress.
She died many, many years ago; but her
niece, when I asked about Nat Bowditch, told
me how her aunt used to love him for his
earnestness in pursuing his studies, and for
his gentleness, while under her care. He was
" a nice boy," she used to say. While in
Danvers, his father was most of the time at

sea, he having been obliged to give up his
trade and become a sailor when the Revolutionary War broke out.* Nat lived, during
his father's absence, very happily with his
mother and his brothers and sisters. During
the whole of his after-life, he used to delight to
go near the small house in which he had dwelt
so pleasantly. The family was "a family of
love." He had a brother William, to whom
he was very much attached. He was more
grave and sober than Nat; for the latter, with
all his devotion to study, was full of fun,

---

* You will know better, by and by, about the Revolutionary War. I will merely state now, that this war was
between America and Great Britain, in order to free our-
selves from the power of England. The reason why the
British King had anything to do with America was this:
Many years ago, a number of people came over from England, and settled in this country; and of course the small
colony needed the aid of the government from which it
originated. After a time the people here wanted to govern
themselves, and they therefore went to battle about it, because England would not grant them all their wishes.
This contest, which lasted for several years, was terminated by the United States becoming free from the power of
Great Britain.

frolic, and good nature. But William was equally, and perhaps more, gentle. The brothers frequently studied together from an old family Bible; and on Sundays, when they were quite small, their grandmother, who was a very excellent woman, used to place this large book, with its wooden covers and bright brazen clasps, upon the foot of her bed; and hour after hour did those two boys trace, with their fingers upon the map, the forty years' wanderings of the Israelites, before they came into the long-looked-for land of Canaan.

I have said that Nat frequently went to look upon the house in which he had lived; and so he often called upon the family in which this old Bible was kept, in order that he might see the volume which he had so loved when a boy. It reminded him of the delightful home of his childhood, where his dear and worthy mother tried to make him good, in order that he might become an honor to her and to the people. His mother was one who was extremely kind; yet she was by no means afraid to correct her children, if she found them doing wrong. Nat sometimes suffered, because, like every boy, he sometimes did wrong; but generally the mother found that he could be easily guided by her love. I seem to see her now, taking her little son, and leading him to the window of the cottage in Danvers, to see the beautiful new moon just setting in the west, while, at the same time, she kisses and blesses him, and talks to him of his absent father, and they both send up earnest wishes for his safe and speedy return. She was very careful to instil into all her children the importance of truth. "Speak the truth always, my boy," said she. She likewise loved religion, and she was very liberal in her feelings towards those who differed from her upon this subject. Nevertheless, believing that the Episcopal kind of worship was the most correct, she educated all her children in that form. An anecdote which Nat, when he became a man, often related, will show you how much influence her instructions in this particular had upon him. Among the Episcopalians the prayers are read, and the people repeat,

aloud, some answer. One day Nat called his
brothers and sisters around him, and, taking
his mother's Book of Prayer, with a sober face
began to read aloud from it, while his brothers made the answers. They had continued
some minutes amusing themselves in this way,
when their mother entered the room. She
was very much troubled at first, as she supposed they were ridiculing the services she
held as sacred. "My sons," said she, "I am
pleased to see you read that book; but you
should never do so in a careless manner."
They told her that, though playing, they did
not think to do any harm, or to show any dis-
respect.

The family was very poor; so poor, indeed,
that sometimes they had nothing to eat, for
several successive days, but common coarse
bread, with perhaps a little pork. Wheat
bread was almost never allowed to any one
of them. Their clothing, too, was at times
very thin. Frequently, during the whole winter, the boys wore their summer jackets and
trousers. At times, Nat's schoolmates used to

laugh at him because he wore such a thin dress, when they were wearing their thickest winter clothing. But he was not afraid of their merriment, nor made angry by it; on the contrary, he laughed heartily at them for supposing him unable to bear the cold. He knew that no good would be gained by complaints, and that he would distress his mother if he made any; he therefore bore contentedly his want of clothing, and tried even to make himself merry with those who ridiculed him.

At the age of seven years, and after returning to Salem, he went to a school kept by a man named Watson. Master Watson was one who had sufficient learning for those times; though the boys who now go to school in Boston would think it very strange if a master did not attempt to teach more than he did. None of the scholars had a dictionary. Master Watson was a good man, but he suffered much from headache, and therefore he was liable to violent fits of anger; and when thus excited, as it generally happens in such cases, he was guilty of injustice. An instance of

this, young Bowditch met with, not long after
he entered the school. From early life, Nat
had liked ciphering, or arithmetic; and thinking that at school he would be able to learn
something more about this than he had previously gained from his brothers, while at
home, during the long winter evenings, he requested the master to allow him to study it.
As he seemed too young, this request was
not granted. But, being determined to study
what pleased him so much, he obtained a letter from his father, in which Mr. Bowditch
requested Master Watson to allow his son to
pursue his favorite study. The schoolmaster,
on receiving the message, was very angry, and
said to his pupil, "Very well. I'll give you
a sum that will satisfy you;" and immediately
prepared a question that he thought Nat would
be unable to answer, and which he could not
have answered had he not studied at home.
But the boy had learned before sufficiently to
enable him to perform the task; and, having
done so, he ran gayly to the desk, expecting
to be praised for his exact performance of

duty. You may imagine his surprise at being saluted with these words: "You little rascal, who showed you how to do this sum? I shall punish you for attempting to deceive me." The poor lad's heart swelled and beat violently. He blushed and trembled from fear of punishment, but still more at the suspicion which his instructor had expressed, that he had been guilty of telling a lie. Filled with anger and alarm, he stammered out, "*I* did it, sir." But his master would not believe him, and was about to strike him, when an elder brother interfered, and stated that Nat knew very well how to perform the task, for he himself had previously taught him enough to enable him to do it. Our young arithmetician thus escaped the punishment; but he never could forget that he had been accused of falsehood. His pious and truth-loving mother had so firmly fastened in his mind the holiness of truth, that he rarely, if ever, thought of deviating from it; and during his life he considered that any one who even suspected him of falsehood had done him the greatest injury.

How well it would be if all of our boys loved truth as he did !

This was the only serious difficulty he met with while at this school. He was the same lively lad at everything he undertook as he had been previously. He was beloved by his comrades for his good nature, and was always engaged in useful employment or innocent amusements. When he was about ten years of age, his father became poorer than ever; and moreover, in consequence of loss of regular employment and of the little property which he possessed, he gave himself up to habits of intoxication. From having been a brave man, he became a coward, and, unable to look at the distress of his family, made their poverty many times more burdensome by habits which wholly unfitted him for active duties. Under these circumstances, his son, at the age of ten years and three months, left school, and soon afterwards was bound an apprentice to Messrs. Ropes and Hodges, who kept a ship-chandler's shop in Salem.

As this was one of the important times in

his life, I think I will finish this chapter with
only two remarks, for the boys and girls who
may be reading this. You see a lively and
good-natured boy, who, before he was ten
years old, showed great love of truth, much
perseverance, a warm desire for study, particularly of arithmetic ; and lastly, you perceive
him under the influence of a good mother,
who tries to excite in him all just and holy
sentiments. Particularly does she point out
to him truth as one grand aim of his existence.
Now, I wish you to remember these facts, and
see where they eventually led him ; and if you
remember, you may be induced to imitate
him, at least in some respects.

CHAPTER II.

From 1784 to 1795 — between the ages of 10 and 21.

His apprenticeship, his habits. — Studies Chambers's Cyclopædia. — Results of his studies; gains the respect
of all. — Dr. Bentley, Dr. Prince, and Mr. Reed, do
him kindness; by their means allowed access to "The
Philosophical Library." — He makes philosophical instruments. — Calculates an Almanac at the age of
fourteen. — Studies algebra: delight he experienced
from this new pursuit. — Learns Latin. — Reads works
by Sir Isaac Newton. — Studies French.

DOUBTLESS it was with a sorrowing heart
that Nat left his own dear home and his kind
mother to take up his abode among strangers;
for he was to live at the house of his employer, Mr. Hodges. But if he did feel sad,
he was not one to neglect a duty in consequence of sorrow. The shop in which he was
employed was situated very near the wharves,

in the lower part of the town of Salem. We do not see many such stores now in Boston; though something similar is sometimes found in small country towns. In it a great variety of goods was sold, especially everything which would be useful to a sailor. Pork and nails, hammers and butter, were kept in adjacent barrels. The walls were hung with all the tools needed in the seafaring life. There was a long counter in it, at one end of which Nat had his little desk. When not engaged with customers, he used to read and write there. He always kept a slate by his side, and, when not occupied by the duties of the shop, he was usually busied with his favorite pursuit of arithmetic. In the warm weather of summer, when there was little business, and the heat was uncomfortable, he was often seen, by the neighbors, engaged in ciphering, while resting his slate upon the half door of the shop; for in those days the shop doors were made in two parts, so that frequently the lower half was shut, while the upper was open. Thus he was always actively employed, instead of being idle, as is too frequently the case with boys in similar circumstances. Even on the great holidays of Fourth of July and "General Training," he did not leave his studies for the purpose of going to see the parade, but remained at the shop, laboring to improve himself; or, if the shop was closed, he was in his little garret-room at his employer's house. Study and reading were beginning to be his only recreation. Frequently, after the store was closed at night, he remained until nine or ten o'clock. Many long winter nights he passed in a similar manner, at his master's house by the kitchen fire. While here, he did not become morose or ill-natured; but frequently, when the servant girl wished to go to see her parents, who lived one or two miles off, he took her place by the side of the cradle of his master's child, and rocked it gently with his foot, while busily occupied at his books. I think this was one of the sweetest incidents in his early days. It was the germ of his benevolence in after-life. A truly great man is kind-hearted as well as wise. Nat began

thus early his course of genuine humanity
and science. So must you do if you would
imitate him.

As he became older, he became interested
in larger and more important works; and of
these, fortunately, he found an abundant supply. His employer lived in the house of
Judge Ropes, and Nat had permission to use
the library of this gentleman as much as he
wished. In this collection he found one set
of books which he afterwards valued very
much. He tried to buy a copy of it when he
was old, having a similar feeling towards it
that he bore towards his grandmother's Bible.
It was Chambers's Cyclopædia. As you may
judge from the name Cyclopædia, these books,
consisting of four very large volumes, contained much upon a great many subjects. It
is like a dictionary. He read every piece in
it, and copied into blank books, which he
obtained for the purpose, everything he
thought particularly interesting, especially all
about arithmetic. Previously, he had studied
navigation, or the methods whereby the sailors

are enabled to guide their ships across the ocean. In this Cyclopædia he found much upon this subject; also upon astronomy, or the knowledge of the stars and other heavenly bodies; and upon mensuration, or the art with which we are enabled to measure large quantities of land or water.

But he was not satisfied with merely studying what others did. He made several dials and curious instruments for measuring the weather, &c. He likewise, at the age of fourteen years, made an Almanac for 1790, so accurately and minutely finished, that it might have been published. Whilst engaged upon this last, he was more than usually laborious. The first rays of the morning saw him at labor, and he sat up, with his rushlight, until late at night. If any asked where Nat was, the reply was, "He is engaged in making his Almanac." He was just fourteen years of age when he finished it.*

---

* It is now in existence, and was kept in his library during his lifetime, and for many years afterwards. His library, at the time of his death, consisted of several thou-

August 1, 1787, — that is, at the age of fourteen, — he was introduced to a mode of calculating which was wholly new to him. His
brother came home from his school, where he
had been learning navigation, and told him
that his master had a mode of ciphering by
means of letters. Nat puzzled himself very
much about the matter, and imagined a variety of methods of "ciphering with letters."
He thought that perhaps A added to B made
C, and B added to C made D, and so on ;
but there seemed to him no use in all this.
At length he begged his brother to obtain for
him the book. The schoolmaster readily lent

sand books, which, during his long life, he had collected.
Yet, to my mind, the little Almanac is the most valuable
book of the whole, because it was the first evidence he gave
of his perseverance, and of the tendencies of his mind. It
is now, with his other manuscripts, preserved in the Public
Library of the City of Boston.

The manuscripts and his whole library were given to the
city when the opening of Devonshire Street, in continua-
tion of Winthrop and Otis Place, required the removal of
the house where they had been preserved from the time of
Mr. Bowditch's death.

it ; and it is said that the boy did not sleep that night. He was so delighted with reading about this method, or algebra, as it is called, that he found it impossible to sleep. He afterwards talked with an old English sailor, who happened to know something about the subject, and received some little instruction from him. This person afterwards went to his own country ; but just before he left Salem, he patted Nat upon the head, and said, " Nat, my boy, go on studying as you do now, and you will be a great man one of these days." You will see, before finishing this story, that the prophecy of the old sailor was amply fulfilled.

But all this labor, this constant exertion, combined with his kind and cheerful disposition, must, you will readily believe, have given him friends. He became known as a young man of great promise ; as one more capable than his elders of deciding many questions, particularly all those in which any calculations were to be made. Consequently, when about seventeen or eighteen years old, he was often called upon, by men much older than himself, to act as umpire in important matters. All these he attended to so willingly and skilfully, that those whom he assisted became very much attached to him. He thus gained the respect not merely of common persons, less learned than himself, but his industry, his fidelity to his employers, his talents, attracted the notice of men well known in the community. Among these were two clergymen of Salem. At the church of Rev. Dr. Prince he attended for divine worship; and Dr. Bentley rarely passed the store without stepping in to talk with his young friend. Nat availed himself of the learning of Dr. Bentley, and often visited his room in order to converse with him. Dr. Prince, the other clergyman above alluded to, had studied much the subjects that the apprentice was pursuing, and he was very glad to see a young man zealous in the same pursuits. There was another individual who kept an apothecary's shop; and it was he, who, with the aid of the two clergymen, opened to our young student the means of con-

tinuing his favorite studies with more success
than he had ever anticipated.   Mr. Reed — for
that was his name — likewise gave him permission to use all his books, of which he had a
great many.   But the chief means of study,
to which I allude, was the permission to take
books from a library which had been formed
by a number of gentlemen of the town.   The
kindness of the proprietors of this library was
never forgotten by the young apprentice ; and
in his will, made fifty years afterwards, he left
a thousand dollars to the Salem Athenæum, in
order to repay the debt of gratitude which he
felt he had incurred.   But you may want to
know something about the formation of this
library, and the books of which it was composed.   Some time during the Revolutionary
War, alluded to in Chapter I., Dr. Kirwan, an
Irishman and a learned man, put the greater
part of his library on board a ship, in order
to have it carried across the Irish Channel.
While on the voyage, the vessel was taken by
an American ship of war, and the books were
carried into Beverly, and were afterwards sold

at auction in Salem. Of all in the world,
these books were perhaps those most needed by
the apprentice. He had been studying those
sciences chiefly, concerning which there were
very few works printed in America ; and sud-
*denly he found himself allowed free access to
all the important books which had been printed
in Europe upon these same subjects. You
may readily imagine how eagerly he availed
himself of the opportunity thus afforded him.
Every two or three days he was seen with a
number of volumes under his arm, going
homeward ; and on his arrival there, he read
and *copied all* he wanted to study at that time,
or refer to afterwards. He made, in this way,
a very large collection of manuscripts, which
formed a part of his library. Thus, by his
own exertions, he, at the early age of eighteen,
became acquainted with the writings of most
of the learned men of Europe ; and he did
this at the time when he was engaged almost
constantly in his store, for he made it a strict
rule never to allow any study or reading,
however interesting, to interfere with his duties

to his employers. He rarely forgot this. The following incident impressed it so strongly upon his memory, that it influenced all his subsequent life.

One day a customer called and purchased a pair of hinges at a time when the young clerk was deeply engaged in solving a problem in mathematics. He thought he would finish before charging the delivery of them upon the books; but when the problem was solved, he forgot the matter altogether. In a few days the customer called again to pay for them, when Mr. Hodges himself was in the shop. The books were examined, and gave no account of this purchase. The clerk, upon being applied to, at once recollected the circumstance, and the reason of his own forgetfulness. From that day he made it an invariable rule to finish every matter of business that he began, before undertaking anything else. Perhaps some of you may remember the story; and when you think of leaving anything half finished, you may repeat to yourselves, " Charge your hinges, and finish what you begin."

Having been instructed in the elements of algebra, Nat soon found that there were books written upon it in other languages, which he knew he ought to read, if he intended to learn as much as he could about algebra. One of these books was written in a tongue which is called a dead language, in consequence of its having ceased to be spoken by the people of the country in which it was originally used. It was in Latin. This language usually requires many years of study, if one wishes to read it well, even when he has good instructors. Our hero, however, never thought of the difficulties he had to surmount, but commenced, alone, the study of it, June, 1790, that is, when seventeen years old. He was soon in trouble. He could not understand his Latin book on mathematics. He asked many who had been at college, but they were puzzled by the peculiar expressions as much as he was. At length, however, by the aid of his friend Dr. Bentley, and afterwards of a German who gave him lessons, he succeeded in mastering the greatest work in modern times, written by Sir Isaac Newton, who, you know, was one of the most famous philosophers who have ever lived in this world. Nat discovered in one part of it a mistake, which, several years afterwards, he published; but he was deterred from doing so at first, because a very much older person than he, a professor in Harvard College, said that the apprentice was mistaken.

But Latin was not the only language that he learned. Finding in the Kirwan library many books upon mathematics written in French, he determined to learn that tongue likewise. Accordingly, at the age of nineteen (May 15, 1792), he began to study it. Fortunately, he was able to make an arrangement with a Frenchman living in Salem, who wished to learn English. Mr. Jordy agreed to teach the apprentice French, on condition that Nat would teach him English. For sixteen months they met regularly, a certain number of times a week; and the consequences were very important to the youth's future success in life. One circumstance took place, during this study of French, which I think it important to mention. Nat, desiring only to learn to *read* a French book, supposed that it would be unnecessary to spend time in learning accurately to *pronounce* the words. These, as is the case in the English tongue, are often pronounced very differently from the manner in which we should be led to speak them, if we judged from their mode of spelling. His master protested against teaching without reference to the pronunciation; and, after much arguing, Nat yielded to the wishes of his instructor, and he studied the language in such a way that he could converse with a Frenchman, as well as read a French book. You will soon see the good that resulted.

CHAPTER III.

From 1784 *to* 1796 — *age,* 10-22.

Apprenticeship continued. — Favorite of his companions.
— Learns music; neglects his studies for a time. —
Gets into bad society; his decision in freeing himself
from it. — Engages in a survey of the town of Salem.
— Sails on his first voyage to the East Indies; extracts
from his Journal during this voyage; arrival at the
Isle of Bourbon; return home.

THOUGH so interested in his studies, Nat
tried, as we have seen, never to neglect a
known duty. Whenever any one came to the
store, he was ready to leave study in order to
attend to him. And he did this cheerfully,
and with so bright a smile that all were
pleased to meet him. His young companions
loved him, for he was not one of those vain
persons who think themselves more important
than others because they are more learned.

On the contrary, what he knew himself he liked to impart to others. He was a member of a juvenile club for the discussion of different subjects. In this association his opinion had much weight, because he rarely spoke, and never unless he had something of importance to say.

Some of his comrades were very fond of music. He had originally a great taste for it. Music, at that time, was less cultivated than it is now; and generally, those who practised it were fond of drinking liquor, and often became drunkards. Nat's love of the flute led him, at times, to meet with several young men of this class. In fact, he was so much delighted with their company, that he began to forget his studies. Day after day he spent his leisure hours in their society; and, for a time, all else was neglected. At length he began to think somewhat in this way: " What am I doing? forgetting my studies in order to be with those whose only recomendation is, that they love music? I shall be very likely to fall into their habits if I continue longer with them. I will not do so." He soon afterwards left their society.

The simple, old-fashioned flute on which he played at these meetings is still preserved. It is a silent monitor to his descendants, urging them to performance of duty, in spite of the allurements of pleasure.

May every boy who reads this remember it, and try, if ever led into temptation as the apprentice was, to say, " I will not," with the same determined spirit that he did.

The time was fast approaching when he was about to leave the business of shopkeeping, and enter upon the more active duties of life. It is true that, to a certain extent, he had been engaged in active life ever since entering his apprenticeship. At the age of ten he had left the home of his mother, and had been obliged to depend much upon himself. His father's habits had finally prevented him from being of service to the family. The mother had died; the family had been broken up; and Nat had thus, at an early age, been thrown upon the world. After having re-

mained with Ropes & Hodges until they
gave up business, he entered the shop of
Samuel C. Ward, which was a similar estab-
lishment; and there he remained until he
was twenty-one years old. He then quitted,
forever, this employment.

In 1794, by a law of the state, every town
was obliged to have an accurate survey and
measurement made of its limits. Captain
Gibaut and Dr. Bentley were appointed by the
Selectmen in Salem to superintend this business. Believing that the calculating powers
of the apprentice would be useful to them,
he was made assistant; and during the
summer of 1794 he was occupied with this
business. Thus we see how his studies
already began to be useful to him. For his
pay, he received one hundred and thirty-five
dollars. Towards the end of the summer, Mr.
Derby, a rich ship-owner in Salem, wished
Captain Gibaut to take command of a vessel
to Cadiz, and thence round the Cape of Good
Hope to the East Indies. Captain Gibaut
consented, and he asked Nat to go with him as

clerk. Nat agreed to the terms; but, owing to some difficulty with Mr. Derby, Captain Gibaut resigned to Captain H. Prince. Young Bowditch was unknown to the latter; but at the suggestion of Mr. Derby, who had heard of the talents and industry of the clerk, the same arrangements were continued by Captain Prince.

A new era in his life was now beginning; and let us look a moment at him. He is now twenty-one years of age. He is already more learned than many much older than himself, in consequence of his untiring industry and his devotion to study and to duty. Yet he is modest and retiring. He is still full of fun and frolic at times, and always ready for acts of kindness. Above all, he is a good youth; no immorality has stained him. His love of truth had been given him by his mother; and since her death he has loved it still more. It is to him a bright light, as it were, to guide him. Cannot we foresee his career?

On January 11, 1795, — that is, when he was a few months more than twenty-one years of age, — he sailed from Salem in the ship

Henry. Though he went as clerk, he was prepared to undertake the more active duties of sailor and mate of the vessel. Thinking that he should be too much occupied to be able to read, he took very few books; and therefore he devoted much more time to observations of the heavenly bodies, the state of the weather, &c., while at sea, and upon the manners and habits of the nations he visited. Though he had not been educated as a sailor-boy, his studies had led him to understand the most important part of a seaman's life, the art of guiding the vessel from one shore to another, across the ocean. In other words, he had studied much on navigation, and copied books upon that subject.

The Journal which he kept during the voyage is quite long. One of the first lines you meet, on opening the book, is the motto which he chose for himself. It is in Latin, and means, that *he would do what he thought to be right, and not obey the dictates of any man.* He notes the events of every day, most of which are similar; but occasionally something unusual occurs.

February 7, 1795, he writes thus : " At ten A. M., spoke a ship, twenty-five days out, from Liverpool, bound to Africa. We discovered her this morning, just before sunrise, and supposed her to be a frigate." They discovered soon that it was a negro slave-ship, and he exclaims thus : "God grant that the detestable traffic which she pursues may soon cease, and that the tawny sons of Africa may be permitted quietly to enjoy the blessings of liberty in their native land."

"February 22. We remember with gratitude that this is the anniversary of the birth of our beloved Washington — the man who unites all hearts. May he long continue a blessing to his country and to mankind at large ! "

During the passage to the Isle of Bourbon, situated, as you know, east of the southern extremity of Africa, he frequently alludes to his native land in terms of respect and love. On May 8, the ship arrived in the harbor of Bourbon. Perhaps you may like to see his description of the town.

" May 9. After dinner, Captain P., Mr. B., and I, went to see the town. It is a fine place. All the streets run in straight lines from the shore, and cross one another at right angles. There is a church here, with a priest to officiate. I went into it. We afterwards went into the republican garden. It is a beautiful place, though at present much neglected. The different walks are made to meet in the centre, and form the figure of a star, each one of the rays of which is formed by thirty-four mango trees, placed from twelve to fourteen feet apart. All the houses of the island are built very low; they have no chimneys. They are two stories high (about ten feet), have lattice windows, outside of which are wooden ones to keep off the sun and rain. The floors are made of the wood of the country, on which they rub wax, as the women of America do on their furniture. It makes them very slippery." There are other places of which he speaks, and in them he finds flower-gardens in abundance, intermixed with groves of coffee and orange trees, &c.

He afterwards alludes to the poor slaves, who, it appeared, suffered as much there as they do in some other places at the present day.

He visits the people of the place, and finds them superstitious and vicious. Alluding to the vice he found there, he writes, "I was reminded of the beautiful words of Solomon, in the Proverbs." This was not the only occasion on which he remembered his Bible; and it seemed always to have a kindly influence over him. On one occasion, several young men argued with him about its truth; and, having heard them patiently, he put his hand over his heart: "Talk no more about it. I know that the Bible is true; that it is capable of doing to me the greatest good. I know so by the feelings I have here."

After remaining in this place until July 25, he set sail for home, and arrived in Salem January 11, 1796, having been absent exactly twelve months.

CHAPTER IV.

From 1796 *to* 1797 — *age*, 23-4.

Second voyage. — Visits Lisbon. — Island of Madeira; festival and games there. — Anecdotes of his skill as an accountant. — Doubles Cape of Good Hope. — Albatrosses. — Arrival at Manilla. — Extracts from Journal. — Curious boat. — Earthquake. — Voyage home.

AFTER remaining at home about two months, he again sailed in the same ship, and with Captain Prince. On the 26th of the following March, they prepared to sail from Salem harbor; but, being prevented by contrary winds from getting out of the bay, the anchor was dropped during the night, and on the following morning, under fair but strong breezes, Mr. Bowditch was again on his way across the wide Atlantic. His course was towards Lisbon, situated at the mouth of

the River Tagus, in Portugal. The first part
of the voyage was unpleasant, because cloudy
and stormy weather prevailed most of the
time; but during the latter part, under pleasant and mild breezes from the south, the ship
rode gayly onwards, and, on the morning of
April 24, the vessel was within sight of
Lisbon, with its beautiful and romantic country behind it. Lisbon is the chief city of
Portugal, and presents a very superb appearance when viewed from a vessel which is entering the harbor. It is the principal com-
mercial place in the kingdom. Its inhabitants
are among the richest. In consequence of its
being the place of residence of the kings of
Portugal, many magnificent country-seats, or
villas, are seen on all the vine-covered hills of
the adjacent country.

The stay at this city was short, and the op-
portunities for visiting the interesting places
in it very limited. Mr. Bowditch seems not
to have been particularly pleased with its appearance. At the time he was there, probably, much less attention was paid to the clean-

liness of the streets than there is now. But
he spent the 28th and 29th of April in walking about the city, and says in his Journal,
that he " found nothing remarkable."

It was at Lisbon that Mr. Bowditch discovered the advantage of having learned to *speak*
French, to which I alluded at the close of the
second chapter. Though a Portuguese port,
the custom-house officers understood French;
and no one on board but he could speak any
other language than the English. The consequence was, that he acted as interpreter, which
was, of course, a great help to the captain.
This incident made a deep impression upon
his mind; and in after-life, when a person in
conversation expressed a doubt about the importance of any kind of knowledge, because
for the time it seemed useless, he would reply,
" O, study everything, and your learning
will, some time or other, be of service. I
once said that I would not learn to *speak*
French, because I thought that I should never
leave my native town; yet, within a few years
afterwards, I was in a foreign port, and I be-

came sole interpreter of the ship's crew, in consequence of my power to speak this language."

On the 30th, having taken on board a quantity of wine, they again were ready for sea; but, owing to bad weather, they did not sail until the 6th of May, when the ship dropped down the river. On the 6th it was on its way to the Island of Madeira, which is a small island, situated about three hundred and sixty miles from the northern part of Africa. At eleven o'clock, May 15, the island was discovered; and, under full sail, the ship swept along the shore until nine in the evening, when they hailed a pilot, who came on board, from the town of Funchal. Mr. Pintard, the American consul of the place, greeted them very cordially. The ship spent six days there, taking in more wine, — for which the country is famous, — and sailed from it on Thursday morning, May 26, 1796. During this residence at Mr. Pintard's, Mr. Bowditch saw some feats of horsemanship, about which you may like to hear. They are thus described in his Journal: "A ring being suspended by a small wire, about ten feet from the ground, at the entrance of the gate of the public garden, a horseman attempted to strike it, and carry it off, while upon full gallop. If he gained the prize, he was attended by the master of ceremonies, mounted on a small colt fantastically adorned with ribbons, &c., with a most deformed mask, who generally gave him a reward fully proportioned to the merit of the action; perhaps a whistle, a small flower, or some little image. During the next day, no business was done by the inhabitants; but the whole of it was devoted to amusements similar to those of the preceding. Again there were masquerades, and some of the richest men in the place joined with the crowd, masked like the people. Others were very richly dressed, like Turks, East Indians, &c. One of them wore a head-dress worth, it was said, forty or fifty thousand dollars." From this description, slight as it is, we may see the difference in the customs between these inhabitants of Madeira and the Americans.

Captain Prince relates the following anecdotes, which occurred during their residence at Madeira. I shall use Captain Prince's words.

"I was one day walking with an American shipmaster at Madeira, who, in the course of conversation, asked me who that young man (alluding to Mr. Bowditch) was. I replied, that he was clerk of the ship under my command, and remarked that he was a great calculator. 'Well,' said the gentleman, 'I can set him a sum that he can't do.' I answered that I did not believe it. The gentleman then proposed a wager of a dinner to all the American masters in port, that he could set him such a sum. The wager was accepted by me, and we repaired to the hotel, where we found Mr. B. alone. The gentleman was introduced, and the question stated to Mr. Bowditch, with the interrogatory, Can you do it? The reply was, Yes. The great sum which had puzzled the brains of the gentleman and all his friends at home, for a whole winter, was done in a few minutes. I remember the question. It was this: To dig a ditch around an acre of land, how deep and how wide must that ditch be, to raise the acre of land one foot?

"One day, Mr. Bowditch and myself received a visit from a Mr. Murray, a Scotchman, who was at that port, having under his charge a valuable cargo of English goods, and who made many inquiries concerning the Americans. He asked particularly what passage we had made against the north-east monsoon, and remarked that it was very surprising that the Americans should come so far, and undertake such difficult voyages, with so little knowledge as they possessed of the science of navigation. In reply to his remark, I told him that I had on board twelve men, all of whom were as well acquainted with working lunar observations for all the practical purposes of navigation, as Sir Isaac Newton would be, should he come on earth. Mr. M. asked how my crew came by that knowledge. I told him, in the same manner that other men came by theirs. He thought it so wonderful, that (as he afterwards told me) he went down to the landing-place, on Sunday, to see my *knowing* crew come on shore. During all this conversation, Mr. Bowditch remained silent, sitting with his slate pencil in his mouth, and as modest as a maid. Mr. Kean, a broker, who was also present, observed to Murray, 'Sir, if you knew what I know concerning that ship, you would not talk quite so fast.' 'And what do you know?' asked Murray. 'I know,' replied Kean, 'that there is more knowledge of navigation on board that American ship (the Astrea) than there has been in all the ships that ever came into Manilla Bay.'"

Mr. Bowditch, during this and the previous voyage, had been in the habit of teaching navigation to the sailors; so that it is probable that, considering the number of persons then on board who really understood practical navigation, Mr. Kean was not so extravagant in his remark as at first sight he seems to be.

May 26, as we have already said, he sailed for India. On July 1, the Island of Trinidad was within sight. They did not stop there, but keeping on their course steadily, two days afterwards crossed the Tropic of Capricorn, in the Southern Hemisphere. On the 17th, during the night, it having rained during the day, the young sailor observed, what we rarely see in this part of the world and on land, but which is not uncommon at sea, a beautiful lunar rainbow. It is caused in the same manner as those rainbows which are seen after a summer shower in the daytime, when the sun is just coming out brightly, and the clouds, which cause the bow to be formed, are passing away afar off in the opposite part of the heavens. But the difference between the solar and lunar rainbows is very great. The solar is grander and has more brilliant coloring, while the lunar bow has a more delicate outline and lighter tints.

August 1, the Journal says, " All the latter part of these twenty-four hours, fine breezes and pleasant, smooth sea. Ever since crossing the Cape [of Good Hope], we have seen a great number of albatrosses, but no fish." These birds are the largest of marine birds. They at times fly and swim (for they are web-footed) to a great distance from land, living upon the fish and other things which may fall in their way. It is said that, as they come gently rising over the waves of the sea, they present a very pleasing sight to the sailor who has been for many months upon the ocean, separated from living things.

For some weeks afterwards, the ship met with severe weather, until September 7, when, according to previous expectation, they saw the land of the Island of Java. The day before their arrival at that place, a curious phenomenon was observed, the account of which I will copy from the Journal. "At seven P. M., the water, as for the two nights past, became of a perfect milk color, through the whole extent of the horizon. We drew a bucket of it in order to determine whether there was anything in it to account for the curious phenomenon. When seen by candlelight, nothing could be observed; but, when carried into a dark place, it appeared full of small, bright, cylindric substances, of the nature of a jelly,

about the size of a small wire, and a quarter
of an inch long. Some large jellies floated on
the water at the same time, and looked like
long pieces of wood. The sky all this time
was perfectly clear; not a cloud to be seen.
About three A. M. the water began to take its
usual color. Next morning we examined the
water which had appeared so shining in the
night; but nothing could be discovered in it,
although it was viewed in a very dark place.
In the forenoon the sea appeared somewhat
colored, of a greenish hue; but some of it, being taken up and carried from the light, appeared colorless."

The next morning the high lands of the
Island of Java came in sight on the horizon,
at the distance of about twenty miles towards
the east. The Journal kept during his passage
through the Straits of Sunda is interesting, because the greatest care was necessary to keep
the ship off from the shoals which abound there.
The current runs at times very swiftly, the
strait being between the large islands of Sumatra and Java, and on the 9th, the force of this

current, and strong head winds, compelled the
captain to cast anchor two or three times.
Finally, on the 17th, the ship was fairly out
of the Straits of Sunda and Straits of Banca,
having been ten days, during sultry weather,
toiling, with much danger, amid coral reefs
and shoals.   The remainder of the voyage
along by the coast of Borneo to the city of
Manilla, the capital of the chief of the Philip-
pine Islands, was more speedy.   At six in the
morning of Sunday, October 2, 1796, the
Island of Luzor was in sight towards the east,
about eighteen miles off.   That same evening
they cast anchor in Manilla Bay, it being a
little more than six months since the sailor
had left his home in Salem.

The following are some extracts from his
Journal while in the city.   Under date of
October 4, he says,   "No coffee can be procured here; the Spaniards, not being very
fond of it, cultivate the cocoa instead.   The
common drink of the natives is sweetmeats
and water, which beverage, they say, is whole-
some and agreeable.   Large quantities of wax

are produced here ; but it is very dear, owing
to the great consumption of it in the churches,
of which there are a great number in Manilla
and its environs.   There are a few bishops in
the island, and one archbishop, whose power
is very great.   The priests are very powerful,
every native wearing the image of the Virgin
Mary, a cross, or some such thing.   No books
are allowed to be imported contrary to their
religion.   The commandant who makes the
visit examines every vessel.   * * * The inhabitants of the city and suburbs are very
numerous, amounting to nearly three hundred
thousand.   In the Philippines there are about
two or three millions.   A great number are
Chinese ; and in general they are a well-made
people.   Their common dress is a shirt, and
trousers, or jackets and trousers.   The women have great numbers of handkerchiefs
about them, so as to be entirely covered.
The natives are well used by the Spaniards,
the King of Spain, in all his public papers,
calling them his children." From these extracts you may judge of Mr. Bowditch's mode

of studying a people when residing with strangers. He afterwards speaks of their games, &c.

The following description of a boat appears on record of October 5: " At twelve, set sail for Cavite in one of the passage-boats, which is very inconvenient for passengers; being nearly three hours before arriving at Cavite, during which time I was basking in the sun. Their boats and manner of sailing are very curious. Having generally light winds, they make their mat sails very large, and the boats, made of the bodies of trees, are very long and narrow; so that there would be great danger of upsetting, if it were not for " out-riggers," which they have on each side, consisting of two bamboos about eight or ten feet long, whose ends are joined to another long bamboo, running lengthwise of the boat. The lee one, on a flaw of wind, sinks a little in the water, and, being buoyant, keeps the boats from up-setting; and on the weather [that is, towards the wind] ones the persons in the boat are continually going out and in, according to the

force of the breeze. In a fresh breeze there
will be six or eight men at the end of the
bamboo, there being ropes leading from the
top of the mast to different parts of the bamboo, to support them as they go. By this
means they keep the boat always upright, and
make it sail very fast, in a good breeze going
five or six knots." After this, a good account
is given of the mode of counting used by the
Malays.

"November 5. About two P. M. there
came on, without any preceding noise, a very
violent shock of an earthquake. It commenced towards the north, and ran very nearly
in a southerly direction. It continued nearly
two minutes; everything appeared in motion.
When it happened, the captain and myself
were sitting reading, and we immediately ran
out of the house. All the natives were down
on their knees, in the middle of the streets,
praying and crossing themselves. It was the
most violent earthquake known for a number
of years. It threw down a large house about
half a league from the city, untiled one of

their churches, and did considerable damage to the houses about the city and its suburbs. Nothing of it was felt on board the shipping."

On Monday, December 12, having sold their wines and laden their vessel with sugar, indigo, pepper, and hides, the party set sail from Manilla, heartily tired with the vices and superstitions of the place. Retracing their course through the Straits of Sunda, with much difficulty they regained the Indian Ocean, and then, setting full sail, they once more looked towards home.

In coming round the Cape of Good Hope, the wind was very favorable. During their passage, several ships were met with, all of whom told them of home, and of the beginning of troubles between America and France, and England. Finally, at six A. M., they saw Cape Ann towards the north-west, and at two P. M., May 22, 1797, the vessel was riding at anchor in Salem harbor, having been about half round the world, and nearly fourteen months from Salem.

CHAPTER V.

From 1797 *to* 1800 — *age*, 24-7.

Marriage. — Third voyage; visits Spain. — Dangers. —
Earl St. Vincent's fleet. — Arrival at Cadiz. — Observatory at Cadiz. — Sails for Alicant. — Passage through
the Straits of Gibraltar. — Privateers; chased by one;
anecdotes of Mr. B.'s love of study shown then. —
Hears news of the death of his wife; consoles himself
with mathematical studies. — More troubles with privateers. — Leaves Alicant. — Advantages derived from his
visit to Spain. — Fourth voyage; to India. — Extracts
from Journal on viewing a ship that was engaged in the
slave trade. — Arrival at Java; introduction to the governor; respect formerly paid to him. — Anecdote of
English navy officers. — Goes to Batavia and Manilla.
— Observations of Jupiter while becalmed near the
Celebean Islands. — Voyage home.

DURING these two voyages, Mr. Bowditch
had been engaged in trade for himself; and
having thereby gained a little property, he
wished to remain at home and enjoy the bless-

ings of domestic life, from which he had been
separated at the age of ten years, when he left
the abode of his parents. In accordance with
this wish, on the 25th day of March, 1798,
he married an excellent and intelligent woman, named Elizabeth Boardman. But in
a few months he was again called to a seafaring life. His young and beautiful wife was
already beginning to show symptoms of that
disease which eventually removed her from her
husband and friends. It was a hard struggle
for the tenderly attached couple to separate;
but duty called the husband, and obedience to
duty was always his watchword. Accordingly,
by August 15, 1798, he was prepared for sea,
in the same ship, with the same owner, Captain Derby, and his friend Captain Prince.
On this occasion he went as joint supercargo.
It was on the 21st of August — nearly five
months from the date of his marriage — that
he bade adieu to his wife. He never saw her
again. Full of devotedness to him, she, however, urged him to do what he thought right,
unconscious that she should never more em-

brace him. During his absence she died at the age of eighteen years.

One of the objects of the present voyage was to go to Cadiz, the chief southern port in Spain. It was rather dangerous at this time for any vessel to sail towards Europe, as the revolution in France had taken place only a short time before, and most of the nations of Europe were beginning to rise against that country; but as Spain was united with France, an English fleet was hovering about the Straits of Gibraltar. The consequence was, that it was of great importance to avoid all vessels, for fear of meeting a privateer.

On the 19th of September, after nearly a month's voyage, they came within sight of the shores of Spain; and at seven A. M. the next day, they discovered the English fleet, under command of Earl St. Vincent, several leagues to the eastward of them. On this same day they were boarded by the captain of an American vessel, who informed them that the privateers were very numerous in the straits.

By Mr. Bowditch's Journal we learn the following : —

"On Thursday afternoon, 20th of September, the winds continued light and variable to the westward. Captain Prince steered directly for Earl St. Vincent's fleet, and at two P. M. the Hector, of seventy-four guns, Captain Camel, sent his lieutenant on board, ordering us to bear down to him. Captain Prince went aboard, was treated politely, and received a passport to enter Cadiz." On the 21st, at four P. M., anchor was cast in that harbor.

The state in which poor Spain was at this time was miserable enough. There was but one newspaper in the whole kingdom, and that was printed at Madrid. Everything was degraded about that once noble and brave-hearted people. Upon the appearance of Cadiz the Journal says thus : " The streets of the city, although narrow, are very neatly paved, and swept every day, so that they are very clean. They have broad, flat stones at the sides. All the houses are of stone, with roofs but little sloping. There are fortifications all around the city."

"September 29, 1798. This day news came of the destruction of the French fleet in the Mediterranean Sea, by Lord Nelson." * Of this event you will read in history at some future time; but it was deemed very important at that time by the whole world. It was one of the most formidable checks received by the French after they had begun to overrun Europe.

This news, of course, was very interesting to our voyager; but, although excited by the political and military contests of the day, he did not forget the subject to which, from earliest years, he had devoted himself. You will perceive from the following extracts from his Journal, that he now was studying astronomy. In fact, he had been reading, during his previous voyages, many of the greatest works on mathematics and astronomy.

---

* This was the famous battle of the Nile. It won for Nelson the title of "Baron of the Nile."

"November 12.   During our residence in
Cadiz we formed an acquaintance with Count
Mallevante, who, before the revolution, commanded a French frigate at Martinico, and at
present is a post-captain in the Spanish navy.
He carried us to the New Observatory, built
on the Island of Cadiz, where we were shown
all the instruments they had mounted.   There
were not any of them very new.   The person
who went with us was named Cosmo de Chur-
ruca.   I promised to send him, on my arrival
in America, the works of Dr. Holyoke on
Meteorology.   I gave him my method of
working a lunar observation, which he was to
print at the end of the Nautical Almanac."

"At half past four P. M., got under way,
and beat out of the harbor of Cadiz, in company with three other American vessels, which
sailed under the protection of the Astræa."
They were destined for Alicante, and consequently their course lay through the Straits of
Gibraltar, up along the south-eastern coast of
Spain.   On the afternoon of the 14th, they
fell in again with the English fleet, which,

with those under their convoy, consisted of forty-five vessels. As the fleet was steering in the same direction, they kept company with it, being all bound for the Straits of Gibraltar. Next day they saw another convoy of twenty vessels, and two of those accompanying the Astræa joined it. The Astræa was obliged to fall behind, because the remaining vessel under its protection sailed too slowly. On the 18th the whole convoy entered the Straits, except one, which was chased by French privateers, ten of which could be counted in full view; but, on the approach of the Astræa, the enemy retreated."

The moon was shining brightly on the night of the 19th of November, 1799. Many times had the bell broken over the silent sea from the ship's deck, telling of the passing hours, when suddenly the crew of the Astræa was called to quarters, for a suspicious sail was seen bearing down towards them. The cannon, of which nineteen were on board, were all cleared for action, and every sailor, placed at his post, watched anxiously as the privateer came rapidly towards them. Captain Prince assigned to Mr. Bowditch a station in the cabin, through which the powder was to be passed to the deck. When all on deck was ready, and that deep and solemn silence which always comes over every part of a ship that is just approaching the enemy, was beginning to creep over those on board the Astræa, the captain stepped for a moment into the cabin to see if everything was in order; and "there sat Mr. Bowditch at the cabin table, with his slate and pencil in hand, and with the cartridges lying by his side." Entirely absorbed with his problem, he forgot all danger, thus showing that his love of science, even when in imminent peril, was superior to all feelings of fear. This anecdote, doubtless, will amuse you. It reminds me of the geometrician Archimedes, who lived two hundred years before Christ, who, as some of you may know, was slain by the soldiers of the Roman General Marcellus, when they sacked the city of Syracuse. Archimedes had labored much for his countrymen during the siege, but finally,

it is said, became so engaged in his studies
that he did not know that the soldiers had
taken possession of the town until they attacked and killed him. Fortunately, in the
case of Mr. Bowditch, no evil ensued. Captain Prince could not restrain himself, but
burst into a loud laugh, and asked Mr. Bowditch whether he could make his will at that
moment; to which question Mr. Bowditch
answered, with a smile, in the affirmative.
Captain Prince adds, "But on all occasions
of danger he manifested great firmness, and,
after the affair of the privateer (which, by the
by, did not molest us), he requested to be sta-
tioned at one of the guns, which request was
granted him."

In this way they continued cruising along
the beautiful Mediterranean, but perpetually
exposed to danger. Now they come within
sight of the high lands of Malaga, and shortly
they fly away from some pirate on the broad
sea. Now they are quietly sailing along
under the warm and sunny skies of an Anda-
lusian climate, and again, in the course of a

few hours, are driven by the current and tempest far away to the south-west. Finally, after a tedious passage, the ship was moored, on Friday evening, November 23, in the harbor of Alicante. After considerable difficulty and delay because the city authorities were afraid of disease being brought into the place by the crews of the ships, they were at length allowed to go on shore. Here melancholy tidings awaited our voyager. By a Salem vessel that had arrived at Cadiz, news came of the death of his wife some time in the preceding October. He made no complaints, however, but quietly sought to interest his mind in his favorite pursuit of astronomy. He always did so whenever any trouble came upon him. In this way he consoled himself, and was not a burden to others by allowing his sorrows to disturb them.

January 24, 1799, having finished loading the ship with brandy, they would have sailed, had not the wind prevented. On February 11th they were still detained by head winds; but now, to their discomfort, they saw a

French privateer cruising off in the bay at the
mouth of the harbor. It was evidently wait-
ing to intrap some one of the American
vessels. On the next day the daring of the
privateer commander arose to such a height,
that he rowed in his barge all around the
American fleet, and insulted some of the
seamen. Towards evening of February 13,
Mr. Bowditch narrowly escaped serious difficulty with them, as the privateer barge and
the American boat coming from shore came
in contact; but the former received the most
damage, and Mr. Bowditch got safely on board
the Astræa. On the 14th, the brigand of the
sea departed, and his ship was soon seen gradually losing itself in the distance over the blue
Mediterranean.

On the next day the convoy sailed. It consisted of five vessels, and by twenty-four
hours of favorable breezes they were brought
within thirty miles of the coast of Barbary;
and, after some trouble in consequence of
being obliged to take in tow those of the convoy which sailed more slowly, the Astræa was

fairly out from the Straits of Gibraltar by February 24, that is, three days from the time of leaving Alicante.

During half the passage home, some of the convoy were in company with them. They had rough seas; but on the 6th of April, at ten o'clock at night, Mr. Bowditch arrived in Salem harbor, having been absent nearly nine months.

This visit to Spain was of service to him in many respects. He there obtained many books on astronomy and navigation, and some celebrated works on history, all of which he studied with care on his voyage home. He, moreover, had gained some knowledge by his visit to the Observatory.

He was not destined to remain at home a long while; but the Astræa having been sold to a merchant in Boston, Mr. Bowditch sailed with Captain Prince from that city on the 23d of the following July, bound for India. It was a long, and to most persons a tedious voyage that he was about to undertake; but to Mr. Bowditch it was the means of improvement. While the ship was sailing quietly along, or sinking lazily from one swell of the sea to another, or being tossed about by the most violent gale, Mr. Bowditch was still laboring at his books. During this voyage, as during the preceding, he did not perform much duty, except when in port, and, consequently, on board ship he had a great deal of time to be devoted to study. And he worthily filled every moment with reading and study to improve himself or others. During this voyage, as in previous ones, he taught the sailors practical navigation. Very few incidents worth mentioning occurred during the voyage; but on the 15th of September, 1799, we find the following in his Journal: "The ship in sight yesterday soon proved to be an English Guineaman. As we came up with him he fired a gun to leeward, which we returned. As we came nearer, he fired one to windward. We returned the compliment and nearly hulled him. When within hail, he ordered our boat out, which Captain Prince refused, telling him to come on board if he wanted anything.   Finally, he requested Captain Prince to haul out our boat, as his was calking, which we could plainly see.   Mr. Carlton went on board with the clearance, and the surgeon came aboard of us, and, after examining our papers and acting in a manner becoming a Guineaman, they made sail."

In order to understand this allusion to the Guineaman, you should know that, at the time we are reading of, the greater part of English merchants, especially those of Liverpool, were engaged in the horrid traffic called the Slave Trade.   Immense numbers of vessels were annually sent from Liverpool and other places in England for the sole purpose of sailing to the coast of Africa, there to get a cargo of the poor natives, whom they carried to the West Indian Islands and America, in order that they might be sold, as slaves, into perpetual bondage.   Men, women, and children, were taken indiscriminately, and crammed together, like bales of cotton or any other goods, between the decks of the vessels.   You may imagine that those who could engage in

such abominable procedings must have lost all
the feelings of humanity. They were used to
blood and rapine; hence you can understand
the reason why Mr. Bowditch uses the term
of reproach that he does. I thank Heaven —
and I feel sure you will agree with me — that,
by the efforts of devoted men and women in
England and elsewhere, that trade has been
formally abolished by Great Britain, and that
every man who now sets his foot on British soil
becomes free. Thank God, also, that our late
civil war has destroyed every vestige of
American slavery, and that we can claim, that
no slave can now breathe on the soil of England or America. But to return to the Astræa.

On December 17 they arrived at Batavia,
the chief city of the Island of Java. The
following will give you some idea of the place
and persons in it :—

"Upon our arrival, after making our report
to the custom-house, we proceeded to the
Saabandar, who introduced us to the governor
and the governor-general, who is command-
er-in-chief, and formerly lived in all the

splendor of an Asiatic monarch. At present the outward marks of respect are far less than they were twenty or thirty years ago. In former times he was attended by his guards, preceded by two trumpeters. Every carriage was forced to stop, and the persons within obliged to dismount, under the penalty of one hundred ducatoons (about one hundred and sixty-seven dollars). Captain —— refused even to stop his carriage, and forced his coachman to drive on. The officers of an English squadron lying at Batavia, in order to show their contempt of the procession, formed a party similar to that attending the governor, only, instead of the aids with their staves, one of the officers bore a staff with a cow's horn tipped with gold, and another an empty bottle. The rest of the officers of the fleet met this procession, and made their respects to it, as the natives did to the governor. At present, all these practices are brought into contempt, so that none now stop for any officers of government."

The Astræa remained but four days at Bata-

via, the captain finding that he could not fill
his vessel with coffee, as he intended. Consequently, after taking a fresh supply of provisions and of water, they weighed anchor, and
bore towards the north, with the intention of
visiting Manilla, as on his second voyage.
Traversing the Straits of Macassar, they
passed slowly up through the China Sea, and
anchored in Manilla Bay on the 14th of February, 1800. During this passage we find
Mr. Bowditch still occupied in the study of
science. When floating, becalmed, among
the islands, during the quiet night, he is
observing the appearance of the planet Jupiter, and studying the motions of its beautiful satellites. As he was thus occupied, he
thought of the immense power of that Being
who first put the bright planet in its appropri-
ate place, and caused it to revolve around our
sun, while its own little satellites, like four
moons, were to keep it company, silently and
grandly, in its mysterious course.

After remaining at Manilla long enough to
get a cargo, the ship was prepared for home.

On the 23d of March it sailed, and during a
passage of six months very little occurred to
interrupt Mr. Bowditch's daily labors. It
arrived on the 16th of September, 1800.
About a fortnight before this, — September 2,
a ship was observed to windward, which
bore down upon them. By the captain they
were informed of the melancholy news (as
Mr. Bowditch says in his Journal) " of the
death of our beloved Washington. Thus,"
continues he, " has finished the career of that
illustrious man, that great general, that con-
summate statesman, that elegant writer, that
real patriot, that friend to his country and to
all mankind ! "

During these different voyages Mr. Bowditch
gained more property. Having obtained, likewise, what was much better, a reputation,
among his fellow-citizens, as a man of great
learning, perseverance, extraordinary skill in
the transaction of business, and unyielding
uprightness, he determined to remain at home.
He therefore bade farewell to the sailor's life,
as he supposed, forever.

CHAPTER VI.

From 1800 *to* 1803 — *age,* 27-30.

Second marriage; character of his wife. — Mr. Bowditch
engages in commerce for two years. — School committee.
— East India Marine Society; a description of the annual meeting of this society. — Mr. Bowditch becomes
part owner of ship Putnam, and sails for India. — Anecdote, occurrence a few days after leaving Salem. —
Studies during the long voyage. — Begins to study and
make notes upon La Place's "Mécanique Céleste." —
Arrival off Sumatra; difficulties there. — Boarded by
English man-of-war. — Revisits Isle of France. — Journal extracts about modes of procuring pepper; seasons
for it, &c. — Incident on approaching Salem harbor. —
Decision of Mr. Bowditch.

On the 28th of October, 1800, Mr. Bowditch married his cousin, Mary Ingersoll. She
was destined to live with him thirty-four
years, and was the source of much of his
happiness in life. She was a person in some

respects as remarkable as her husband. She was possessed of excellent judgment, unwearying kindness and love. She had also an elastic cheerfulness which scarcely anything could subdue, and very strong religious feelings. She was constantly trying to aid him. Instead of seeking for enjoyment in display, she preferred economical retirement, and great but respectable frugality, in order that her husband might pursue more thoroughly and easily his favorite studies, and might purchase books of science. Instead of collecting beautiful furniture, she called her visitors to see the new works of learning that her husband had imported from foreign lands. Yet, with all this devoted love, with all this reverence for his talents and virtues, she remained his true friend, and never shrunk from fully expressing her own opinion upon every matter of duty; and if, perchance, she differed from him, she maintained her side of the question with the zeal of a saint. It has been often said, that, had Mr. Bowditch been united with a woman of a different temperament, he would have been an entirely different person. He loved study, it was true; but none enjoyed more than he the delights of a family circle. None needed more than he did the kindness of a wife and children. She lived with him thirty-four years, and on the 17th of April, 1834, she died of consumption, after long and severe suffering.

But I am anticipating my story. For two years after his arrival from his last voyage, Mr. Bowditch remained at home, and engaged as a merchant in commerce. We find him generally, in connection with his old friend Captain Prince, trying his fortunes by adventures of money sent to different parts of the world. In 1802 he owned one sixth of a small schooner and its cargo, valued at nine hundred and eleven dollars. During this long residence in town, his fame had increased. He had become known among his fellow-citizens as an "able mathematician." * He

* From Rev. Dr. Bentley's manuscript Journal.

was therefore appointed to offices of honor
and trust. He was a member of the school
committee of the town. This boy, who had
been obliged to leave school at the age of ten
years and three months, was now, at the age
of twenty-five years, appointed to superintend
the instruction of others. He was secretary
of the East India Marine Society of Salem.
This society had one of the most interesting
collections of East Indian curiosities that can
be found in America. It is now in the possession of the Essex Institute. The East
India Marine Society was composed of the
most influential men in Salem. No one could
be enrolled among their number unless he had
sailed, as captain or supercargo of a vessel,
around either Cape Horn or the Cape of Good
Hope. It was intended as a benevolent society, for the relief of the families of deceased
members, and also for the promotion of the
art of navigation. Mr. Bowditch was one of
its most active members. In the early part
of this century, the society was accustomed,
on the days of its annual meeting, to have a

public procession. A description of one of these processions may not be uninteresting to you. I quote the words of an eye-witness [*] of a celebration that occurred two years later than the period of which I am speaking; but the date is unimportant, as the ceremony was the same. " January 4, 1804. This day was the annual meeting of the East India Marine Society. As the clergy attend in turn, this occasion afforded me an opportunity to enjoy the day with them. After business, but before dinner, they moved in procession, but the ice limited the distance. Each of the brethren bore some Indian curiosity, and the palanquin was borne by negroes dressed nearly in the Indian manner. A person dressed in Chinese habits, and masked, passed in front. The crowd of spectators was great. Several gentlemen were invited to dine. Instrumental music was provided in the town, for the first time, and consisted of a bass drum, bassoon, clarinet, and flute (!), and was

[*] Dr. Bentley's Journal, above cited.

very acceptable. There was no singing."
* * * "It is a most happy arrangement,"
continues this writer, "to deliver all the
papers of this company into the hands of Mr.
Nathaniel Bowditch, lately returned from his
voyage to India, that they may be prepared for
public inspection."

In July, 1802, Mr. Bowditch bought a part
of a small vessel engaged in a sealing voyage;
but he lost, by this adventure, half of his in-
vestment. In September of the same year,
he, with three others, bought the new ship
Putnam, built a short time previously, at
Danvers. This purchase probably caused a
change in his determination of never going to
sea again.

On the 21st of November he sailed as master, and owner of one small part of the whole
ship and cargo, valued at fifty-six thousand
dollars. Though he went in the capacity of
captain, he was determined to do nothing more
than direct the course of the ship. He meant
to leave to the officers under him all the labor
usually expected of commanders. He made

an agreement with two skilful persons to take upon themselves these duties. He did so in order that he might be able to pursue his studies more uninterruptedly than would have been possible, had he been obliged to watch every favorable breeze, or the first appearance of a gathering storm. But, as we shall see, whenever real danger called him to duty, he then stood firm, and gave his commands like one who was satisfied that the time had come for him to do so. A few days after leaving the port of Beverly, he was seen walking " fore and aft " the vessel, with rapid steps, and deeply absorbed, apparently, in the solution of a problem. The wind had been blowing freshly for some time ; and, while he was meditating, and forgetful of everything else, the mate of the vessel had been hoping that he would see the severe squall which was threatening, and was, even then, skimming fiercely over the troubled water. He feared to suggest to Mr. Bowditch the importance of taking in sail, because the discipline on board ship prevents an inferior officer from interfering with the superior, when the latter is on deck. At length, aroused by the danger of the vessel, he ventured the remark, " Captain, would it not be better to take in the topgallant sails?" These words aroused Mr. Bowditch from his reverie, and he instantly ordered all hands to duty, and fortunately, by his activity and energy, was enabled to furl the extra sail before the gust struck the vessel. But this event taught Mr. Bowditch a lesson; and he gave strict orders to the two officers mentioned above to waive all ceremony with him, and to take the command of the ship whether he was on deck or not. This rule was afterwards always observed, except on difficult occasions; and then Mr. Bowditch assumed the authority of commanding officer. On these occasions, by his calmness and sagacity he gained the respect and confidence of those in employment under him. Before the termination of this voyage, we shall see a striking example of this. But now let us proceed on our expedition with him, and again cross the Atlantic, pass around the Cape of Good Hope to the islands of the Indian Ocean. But I should premise, that, as he had become more acquainted with mathematics and philosophy, he had imported from Europe most of the great works on these subjects; and he now was prepared to devote himself more closely than ever to the darling object of his life — the attainment of a knowledge of the truths of science. He was determined, on this voyage, to undertake the thorough study of one work on the heavens — a book which he had understood was above anything ever before written by man on that subject. Imagine, if you can, the zeal and delight with which he must have approached this book upon a subject that had interested him from earliest years. Doubtless he thought not, then, of the fame he was to gain from it. The name of it you will like to know. I shall speak of it again; but, meanwhile, I will merely mention that it was called " A Treatise on the Mechanism of the Heavens," — *Mécanique Céleste*, — and was written, in French, by a mathematician named La Place, the greatest scientific man, after

Newton, of modern times. But this was not the only work Mr. Bowditch took with him. He had many of the most important works which had been published on the same subject, they having been imported for him by a bookseller named Blunt, in payment of services rendered.

These various studies of course influenced his Journal. He was an observer of passing events; but he recorded less of them than on the preceding voyages.

By the first record, it appears that on "Sunday, November 21, 1802, at one o'clock P. M., sailed from Captain Hill's wharf, in Beverly. At two, passed Baker's Island lights, with fine and pleasant breeze." This fair weather lasted but a few days, and by far the greater part of the voyage was uncomfortable, in consequence of the prevalence of rain and wind. On January 25, 1803, he saw the islands of Tristan d'Acunha, and, whilst coursing along under easy sail, took several observations of them, and made a chart of their various positions.

On the 2d of May he arrived among the
Pepper Islands, near the coast of Sumatra.
He found several American captains there, all
actively engaged in loading their vessels with
pepper. He had considerable difficulty in
making any arrangement with the Rajahs of
different places; but at length, having touched,
without success, at several ports, he began to
load at Tally-Poo, on the 9th of May. There
he continued until the 18th of July, when, by
his Journal, it appears that, having wasted a
number of days, expecting that more pepper
would be brought to the shore, he at last was
informed by the Rajah he would not be allowed
any more. Knowing that he should meet
with equal trouble at every place on the coast,
he concluded to quit it, and call at the Isle of
France on his homeward passage. During
their voyage, amid the various shoals and
islands which abound here, they met with no
inconvenience and no interruption, save that
they anchored once or twice, towards night,
and on the 25th of July were obliged to
heave to, under the fire of two English ships

of war, one named the Royal George, the commander of which took the liberty of searching, for the purpose of seeing whether there were any Englishmen on board.* The officer on this occasion was very polite, and the Putnam soon resumed its course, and in seventy-two hours more was on the open sea, under full sail, with the aid of the steady trade-winds of that place and season. On the 24th of August the vessel was in sight of the Isle of France. He there met his old friend Bonnefoy, whom he had left there on his first voyage, in 1795, and likewise many American friends. After purchasing some bags of pepper, and taking on board some provisions, which employed his time for four days, he sailed, for the last time from any foreign port, on Wednesday, August 31, 1803. The voyage homeward was very disagreeable, in consequence of much severe weather. Nothing remarkable happened to enliven the scene;

---

* This and similar acts committed by Great Britain were the prominent causes of the war between the United States and England in 1812.

but Mr. Bowditch disregarded the storms and
waves.   His mind was calm and tranquil, for
he was daily occupied with his "peaceful
mathematics."   He wrote in his Journal but
seldom.   There is, however, the following
account of the Pepper Islands.   "There are
several native ports on the north-western coast
of Sumatra, where the Americans trade for
pepper — Analaboo-Sooso, Tangar, Tally-Poo,
Muckie, &c., and several smaller ports, in-
cluding about fifty miles of the coast.   On
your arrival at any of these ports, you con-
tract with the Datoo for the pepper, and fix
the price.   If more than one vessel is at the
port, the pepper which daily comes to the
scales is shared between them, as they can
agree, or they take it day by day, alternately.
Sometimes the Datoo contracts to load one
vessel before any other one takes any, and he
holds to his agreement *as long as he finds it
for his interest, and no longer;* for a hand-
some present, or an increase in the price,
will prevent any more pepper from being
brought in for several days; and the person

who has made the agreement must either quit
the port or offer an additional price.

" The pepper season commences in January,
when they begin to take from the vines the
small kernels at the bottom. In March,
April, and May is the height of the crop, at
which time the pepper taken from the top of
the vines is larger and more solid than that
gathered at an earlier period. Many suppose
that the pepper is all gathered in May; but I
was in some of the gardens in July, and found
at the top of the vines large quantities which
would be ripe in a few days. The young crop
was in considerable forwardness at the bottom
of the vines. Some calculate on two crops,
but from the best information I could procure
there is only one.

" The pepper is generally weighed with
American scales and weights, one hundred and
thirty-three and a third pounds to a *peccul*.
What is weighed each day is paid for in the
evening, the natives not being willing to trust
their property in the hands of those they
deal with. And they ought to be dealt with

in the same manner, it not being prudent
to pay in advance to the Datoo, as it would be
often difficult to get either the pepper or the
money again from him. Spanish dollars are
the current coin, but they do not take halves
or quarters. They have a pang or piece, of
which we could get but eighty for a dollar at
Tally-Poo, though at other places they give
one hundred or one hundred and twenty for
the same."

During the whole voyage, as I have already
stated, the weather had been very uncomfortable. The approach to the American coast
is at all times hazardous during the winter.
The bold and rocky shore, the intense cold
and severe snow-storms, which make the day
shorter even than common, are so many terrors
for the sailor. You may judge of the anxiety
of the crew of the Putnam, when, after a
tedious absence of more than a year, they at
length, towards the middle of December,
1803, after a long period of stormy weather,
came upon the shoal grounds off Massachusetts near Nantucket. The sleet and rain

had been driving over the ocean for many days. No sun appeared to guide them by day; no star lighted up the night. Groping, as it were, in darkness, they coasted along up the shore, yet not within sight of it, now throwing their sounding-line upon Nantucket, and soon afterwards upon George's Shoal. There seemed no end to the storm. At length, on the 25th of December, they had approached, according to Mr. Bowditch's reckoning, from observation made two days before, near to the outer part of Salem harbor. The night was fast closing in. Mr. Bowditch was observed to be on deck, anxiously looking towards the bow of the vessel, as if trying to see something that would enable him to know more exactly the position of the vessel and the precise course it was running. With clear and decided tones, he gave his orders. The seamen heard him, and obeyed promptly. "There is something in the wind," whispered one; "the *old man* * is above." "Stand every

* An expression of which sailors make use when speaking of the captain of the vessel, and on this occasion over-

man at his post," is the command; "and look out for land ahead." Fierce gusts of wind swept over Massachusetts Bay, bearing the vessel irresistibly onwards. The snow-storm beat heavily, and at every moment the darkness increased. At length, for a moment, the clouds of drifting snow-flakes parted, and Mr. Bowditch and his mate, who were watching, saw distinctly the light of Baker's Island. "Light, ho! on the larboard bow," was passed from one to the other on board that ship, in which were many almost breathless with suspense. It was but for a moment, and again all was obscured. "I am right," said Mr. Bowditch; "the direction in which we are now steering will carry us soon into Salem harbor." His prediction was fulfilled, and it was an extraordinary proof of his skill in navigation. He had had no opportunity for observing the sun or moon for two or three days; yet, so accurately had he marked his position in the ocean at the last time of observing, that, by steering in the

heard by Mr. Bowditch, as two sailors whispered one to another, as they passed him on the deck.

direction pointed out by the chart, and observing the rate at which the vessel moved, he had been able to calculate so exactly, that, after seventy-two hours of darkness, as it were, he came up within sight of the light-house almost as easily as if he had been steering in open day, with the object distinctly in view. The old tars could not restrain their expressions of admiration; and as, at nine o'clock in the evening, they dropped anchor in safety from the gale that was now beating with tenfold violence outside of the island, they whispered with one another, so that he overheard them, " The *old man* has done well to-night." It was the 25th of December, and throughout Christendom the Christmas festival in commemoration of the birth of the Saviour had been celebrated, and friends had all been gathered. Sadness marked their countenances at one home, from which the husband and friend was absent, though long expected. As the blasts beat through the streets, and as the family clustered around the bright, shining fire upon the hearth-stone, as the wind whis-

7

tled through the casement, the thoughts of
the wife were turned from the fireside to the
rough ocean on which her husband was tem-
pest-tossed.   Many weary weeks had she
watched; but day after day had the sun gone
down, and, like Rachel, she could not be com-
forted.   She feared that he was lost.   One
after another of her friends had left her late
at night, and finally she was alone.   Suddenly
she springs up from her seat, aroused by the
sound of quick knocking at the street door.
She recognizes the tap, and in a few moments
she is hanging on his neck from whom she
was destined never to be long separated, until
death removed her from him for four years,
at the end of which time he was placed by
death in quietness at her side.

CHAPTER VII.

Review of the labors, &c., performed by Mr. Bowditch, during these voyages. — Habits while at sea; studies; desire to teach others; kindness to sailors and to the sick. — Discovers errors in a book on navigation. — Origin of " American Practical Navigator; " success of it; industry of Mr. Bowditch upon it. — Investigates higher branches of science. — " Mécanique Céleste." — Mr. Bowditch reads history. — Learns Spanish, French, and Portuguese languages. — Anecdotes. — Chosen member of American Academy. — Receives honors from Harvard College.

THUS finished Mr. Bowditch's career as a sailor, after he had been about eight years engaged in this pursuit. Let us now review a little, and see what he was doing during these voyages, and how he occupied his time. He was very regular in his habits. During the first two voyages he attended to the duties of mate of the vessel. This, of course, pre-

¬vented him from studying as much as he oth-
erwise would have done.   He, moreover, as
we have seen, took fewer books with him.
But during the next two voyages, the captain
excused him from the watches, and he was
able to read with less interruption.   After
the deck had been washed in the morning, he
walked for half an hour.   He then went into
the cabin to study, until the time arrived at
which he was to observe the sun.   This was
done every day at noon, in order to tell
whereabouts in the ocean a vessel is at the
moment of the observation.   Having finished
this, he usually dined.   After this he slept a
few moments, or took a walk, and then
studied again until tea time.   After supper he
was again at work until nine, when he used to
walk for some time, cheerfully talking with
his comrades.   Afterwards he usually studied
until late at night ; and in order not to disturb
his fellow-passengers, he did not keep a light
in the cabin, but frequently stood upon the
cabin stairway, reading by the light of the
binnacle lamp, where the compass was kept.

Whenever the vessel arrived at a port, he was still engaged, but in a different way, perhaps. The instant he was freed from the duties of weighing pepper on the coast of Sumatra, he went to his books. No time was wasted, either in foul or fair weather. It made no difference to him whether the ship was resting motionless upon the water, or tossing upon the heaviest swell, he was always a worker. But there was yet another and still more pleasant trait in his character. He not only loved study himself, but he was determined to persuade all others to love it also. During his first voyage, he used to go to the forecastle, or sailor's cabin, and carry his books of navigation, and teach the seamen how to guide a ship by the rules found in these books. He then went on deck, and explained to each one the method of using the quadrant and sextant, two instruments used by a sea captain. There was an old man formerly living in Salem, who, when speaking of this disposition of Mr. Bowditch, said, "I was the steward on board the vessel, and Mr. Bowditch frequently scolded me because I did not come to study with him more steadily." It is a fact that every sailor on board the ship during that voyage became afterwards captain, and probably some of them would never have risen so high, had it not been for the kindness of their friend. I like to think of this trait in his character. He delighted in learning for its own sake, and he was always pleased when he could find some one upon whom he could bestow all his acquirements. He had no mean standard of comparison between himself and his fellows, but desired to give and receive as much good as it was possible for him to bestow or accept.

He was beloved for this by all; but his kindness of heart led him not merely to teach those who knew *less* than he, but he did all he could to relieve them when ill. One of them wrote in a letter answering my inquiries, after alluding to Mr. Bowditch's willingness to teach others, "But the kindness and attention to the poor seasick cabin-boy are to this day [April, 1838] uppermost in my memory, and will last

when his learning is remembered no more."
He might have been as learned, without dis-
playing this regard for others. But he would
not then have had such tributes of love as
was displayed by this old sailor, who remembered his kindness rather than his instruction.

But let us examine his particular studies
pursued while at sea. We have already seen
that from a boy he had liked simple arithmetic, and on becoming older had studied deeply
into mathematics — a kind of learning similar
in character to arithmetic, only much more
difficult and important. During the long voyages to India, he had ample opportunity for
following this branch of science ; consequently
we find that he was chiefly occupied with that
subject. On the first voyage he discovered
many errors in a book on navigation, some of
which were so important, that in consequence of
them, not a few vessels had been shipwrecked.
This erroneous work was originally published
in London, by a man named Hamilton Moore,
and it was almost the only one in use among
seamen. It had been reprinted in America,

in 1798, by Mr. Blunt, then living in New-buryport. One edition had been published, and a second was about to be issued, in 1799, when Mr. Blunt learned, by means of a mutual friend, that Mr. Bowditch, during his two first voyages, had detected many of these errors, and was willing to inform him of them. Mr. Blunt immediately made application to the young navigator, and received the assistance he wanted. Finding that Mr. Bowditch had within him the means of rendering essential service, Mr. Blunt proposed to him, when starting on his fourth voyage, — that is, to India, — to examine all the tables, and see what number of errors he could find. Mr. Bowditch agreed to the proposal, and during this voyage his time was much occupied with this task — a very wearisome, but, as it proved eventually, a profitable one, as it regards reputation and pecuniary success. The mistakes were so numerous that he found it much easier to make a new work, and introduce therein his own improvements; so that Mr. Bowditch, before the termination of the voyage, decided to make some arrangement for this purpose. The consequence was, that, instead of publishing a third edition of Moore's Navigator, in 1802, the first edition of the "American Practical Navigator" was published by Mr. Bowditch, under his own name, Mr. Blunt being proprietor. Thus was laid, at the age of twenty-nine, the foundation of a work on navigation that has kept constantly before the public, as one of the best of the kind, either in America or England. It passed through its tenth edition a short time before Mr. Bowditch's death.* It soon superseded entirely Mr. Moore's, and was early republished in London. And it was not only obtained by every American seaman, but even English ships sought for Bowditch's Navigator as their safety during their long voyages. Many amusing anecdotes are related in reference to this book.

---

* It is still (1869) used in the American, and often in the English marine service. The twenty-eighth edition was only recently published; about seventy-five thousand copies have been issued since the first edition was printed under the special direction of Mr. Bowditch.

An American captain once took passage in an English ship from the Isle of France for St. Helena. After being a few days out, the passenger, about noon, brought on deck his "Navigator" (one of Bowditch's editions) for the purpose of using it. While thus engaged, the English captain of the vessel walked up and looked at the work. "Why," says he, "you use the same work that we do. Pray, where did you get that?" And great was the surprise of the Englishman, when he learned that the author of the book he was using every day of his life was the near neighbor and friend of the person he was talking with. Little did he imagine that he was dependent upon the efforts of a son of an American cooper for the information by which he was enabled to go from sea to sea in comparative safety. But how is it that this work has been able to remain so long one of the best works of the kind? Because Mr. Bowditch bestowed very great pains upon it, and with every new edition made all the improvements possible. He moreover brought all his learning to bear upon it. To use a common phrase, he put, for the time being, his "whole heart into" making it as perfect as possible. In the explanations of the rules he was simple, so that the most ignorant could understand them. But, in addition to all this, as we have already stated, he introduced all the new methods which he himself had discovered. One of these was favorably noticed by a celebrated French astronomer, in a Journal published in 1808.

But, although his attention was much devoted to this book on navigation, he evidently considered it as of little moment, compared with more important objects. During the long voyages he had been studying the higher branches of the mathematics and their applications to the calculation of the motions of the heavenly bodies. The interest he felt in these pursuits had a most pleasing effect upon him. If he were sad or disturbed, he found quiet and cheerfulness in "his peaceful mathematics." As arithmetic had been the darling pursuit of his boyhood, so now the curious and intricate problems of mathematics, and the sublime theories of the planets, occupied his best leisure hours. We have seen that, long before going to sea, he studied French for the purpose of reading a work on mathematics. He continued to read with much interest the works of that country. Some of you may know that about the close of the last century, at the revolution in France, all the nation was aroused; every branch of learning and of art received new life. The consequence was, that many men of the highest genius arose, and, being patronized by government, they put forth to the world extraordinary works of learning. Most of these, when upon astronomy, Mr. Bowditch procured for himself, by means of the publisher of the "Navigator." He was still engaged in extracting from various works, or, in other words, in filling up his volumes of manuscripts, though now, from the increase of his property, he was enabled to buy the originals; and of course his manuscripts were chiefly his sea journals, and the notes made by himself upon the various au-

thors he read. But he did not confine himself
entirely to science. He read history, and
some works of a literary character, but he
never spent much time upon inferior books.
" Why read anything you cannot speak of?"
he used frequently to say. He likewise
studied the Spanish, Italian, and Portuguese
languages.

His mode of learning languages is instruc-
tive. As soon as he determined to study one,
he bought a Bible, Grammar, and Dictionary
in that tongue. After learning a few of the
pronouns and auxiliary verbs, he began to
translate, and usually commenced with the
first chapter of the Gospel of St. John, because in the few first verses there are many
repetitions. Having studied them thoroughly,
he proceeded to other portions of the Bible,
with which he was most acquainted. He always carried to church a Bible in the language
he was studying, and used it, instead of
an English one, during the services. But
he had another plan, which is very useful
to one who has a bad memory. I will

now explain to you one of his vocabularies, or collections of words, with their meanings attached thereto, so arranged that he could refer much more easily to them than to a common dictionary. He did not learn German until a long time after the period of his life of which we are now speaking; but as the German vocabulary is the most perfect, I will describe it. It is made upon two large sheets, one foot broad, and more than a foot and a half high, which, with the inside of the covers, make six pages. The pages are divided into columns about one and a half inches wide, that is, large enough to admit, in very small writing, a word with its signification by its side. Of course the columns are divided for the letters of the alphabet, in a manner proportioned to the number of pages of each letter in the dictionary. Having thus prepared his book, whenever he found that he was obliged, for want of memory, to look at the dictionary more than once for the meaning of a word, he wrote it in his vocabulary, and, by the act of writing, strengthened in some

measure his memory of that word; and, moreover, he could find it immediately, and not
lose time as in turning over the leaves of a
larger book. The number of words thus seen
at a glance, as it were, is remarkable. In the
above-described six pages, there are eleven
thousand German words, all written distinctly,
but in small letters, and without any repetitions, and with as many abbreviations as he
himself chose. I have been thus minute upon
this subject, not because I think that all ought
to make vocabularies, but because some may
be benefited by so doing. Moreover, I wished
to speak to you of them as proofs of his perseverance.

Two important events took place during this
period of Mr. Bowditch's life, which it becomes our duty to record. On the 28th day
of May, 1799, he was chosen a member of
the American Academy of Arts and Sciences.
This society was the first which bestowed
upon him the honor of membership of its
body. It is composed of men of science,
combined for the purpose of improving them-

selves and the community in knowledge. He continued a member of this body during his life; and in May, 1829, just thirty years after becoming a member, he was chosen its president, in which office he was continued until the day of his death.

Another honor, and one which was more pleasant to him than any received at any time afterwards, was bestowed during this period. In 1802 his ship was wind-bound in Boston, and he left it for the purpose of attending the annual commencement at Cambridge College. He knew but few individuals there, though he had corresponded with some of the professors; and one of the corporation of the college, Chief Justice Parsons, was one of his kindest friends. He went alone, and, while listening in the crowd to the names of those upon whom the honors were conferred, he thought he heard his own pronounced; but he supposed that he might have been mistaken, inasmuch as the notice was given in Latin. But how great was his emotion, when he heard from a friend that his suspicions were well founded! It was to him the proudest day of his life. And we, who know his humble origin, his simplicity and modesty, can in some measure understand the thrill of pleasure that ran through him, when he found himself thus noticed by the first and oldest university in the land. And why was he thus noticed? Because he had well improved the hours of his life; because his days and nights had been spent in activity and earnest study. In after-life, when his fame was established, and the great societies of Europe bestowed upon him their diplomas, he always looked upon them as of small moment, compared with this his first, earliest proof of esteem from his fellow-men. I will take this opportunity to state that very many years afterwards he was elected one of the corporation of the college. This he deemed his highest honor, and his estimate was a just one, for it placed him among the select few who manage the whole affairs of the university — a place doubtless coveted by many, but to which few are called.

8

Having now completed his sea life, let us enter upon his new scene of energy and benevolence as a citizen and father; and our next chapter will include several years of his residence at Salem.

CHAPTER VIII.

From 1803 *to* 1817 — *age*, 30-44.

Mr. Bowditch translates a Spanish paper; is chosen president of a Fire and Marine Insurance office. — Habits of life. — Becomes interested in politics. — Federalists and Democrats. — Great excitement. — Division between him and old friends in consequence of his zeal. — Feelings of Mr. Bowditch when war was declared. — Decision of character. — His charity. — Earnestness in aiding others; ludicrous instance of the effects of this. — Boldness towards a truckman. — Zeal for improving the libraries; unites the two. — Dr. Prince's church. — Performance of duties of president of Insurance Office. — Answer to an overbearing rich man. — Appointed professor of mathematics at Harvard College; same at West Point. — His modesty. — Hints about leaving Salem.

MR. BOWDITCH, on his arrival from sea, met with one of those events to which he always referred when any one doubted the expediency of any kind of knowledge. In his voyages to Portugal and Spain, he had become acquainted with the Spanish language. It so happened that no one else in Salem was acquainted with it, and an important paper came to the care of a sturdy and sensible old sea captain; but it was unfortunately unintelligible to him, for it was written in this same unknown tongue. A friend suggested to him that probably Mr. Bowditch would decipher it for him. The document was handed to Mr. Bowditch, who in a few days returned it with a free English translation accompanying it. The old sailor was delighted, and immediately supposed that any one who knew so much about a foreign language must be a very superior person, and capable of performing any duties. Moreover, he was delighted with the apparent generosity of Mr. Bowditch, in making the translation without charge to his employer. It happened at this time that an insurance office in Salem was in need of a president. The captain was one of the directors of this institution, and used all his influence in promoting the election of his young friend. This influence succeeded, and in 1804, when he was thirty-one years old, we find Mr. Bowditch installed as president of the Essex Fire and Marine Insurance Company. In this office he continued, with entire success, until 1823, when he removed to Boston, and took charge of other similar but much larger institutions. The relief was great which he experienced from not being obliged to seek subsistence for his family by continuing in the sailor's life. The duties of the office in which he now engaged *seemed* to occupy all his time; yet he did not neglect science. He arose at six in the morning during the year, and took a walk, either before or after breakfast, of at least two miles. Afterwards he studied mathematics until nine, and he then went to the office, where he continued until one. After another walk he dined, and after a short sleep he again visited his office until tea time. From tea time until nine in the evening he was at the same place occupied with business. He was not, however, all the time, during office hours,

actually engaged in the necessary work incident to his position as president; but he was
constantly liable to interruption, as much as he
had been when an apprentice. Yet he found
leisure enough for study by early rising and
by regular habits. He used to say, " Before
nine o'clock in the morning I learned all my
mathematics." He kept some of his books on
science at his office, and whenever a moment
of leisure occurred, spent the time in reading
them. At home he had no private room
for many years; and, as his family of young
children grew up around him, he studied
at his simple pine desk, in the midst of
their noise and play. He was never disturbed, except when they failed in kindness to
one another, and then he could never work
until quiet was restored. In truth, the influence of his studies was felt by his children,
whose greatest reward was to receive from
him, in token of his approbation, the drawings
of various constellations upon their arms or
forehead. It was a sad day for them when
they did not receive from his pen the repre-

sentation of the Belt of Orion, the Great Bear, or of some other beautiful constellation in the heavens.

But, in addition to the duties of his office, he became interested in the political affairs of the day. After the revolution, and the new government of the country went into operation under the presidency of General Washington, there had been but little political excitement in Essex County. There were no great parties, which were destined soon afterwards to spring up and excite the bitterest animosity between individuals who had been from birth the warmest friends. It would be impossible, were it useful, to tell all the causes that led to the formation of the two great sects in politics, called the Federalists and Republicans. Suffice it to say, that even during Washington's connection with the government, the seeds of this division were beginning to spring up, and, upon the accession of John Adams, as his successor, the political rancor between these two parties increased with tenfold energy, until at length the

republican party triumphed in the election
of Thomas Jefferson to the office of President
of the United States.   In Salem the violence
of party spirit rose as high as in any city of
the Union.   It would have been surprising,
with his desire for aiding any public cause, if
Mr. Bowditch had not been influenced by the
excitements of the day.   We frequently find
at the bottom of a page, or at the end of some
theorem, brief memoranda of the results of an
election.   He was, moreover, for two years a
member of the State Council.   He was likewise proposed by the Federalists as a repre-
sentative to the General Court, but at that
election they were defeated.

We have scarcely any idea of the violence
with which the two parties contended.   Persons who had been, during life, sincere and
devoted friends, were separated by this viru-
lence.   Mr. Bowditch suffered as much as
others on this account, and two of his longest
and best-tried friends he did not have any
intercourse with for many years.   Dr. Bentley and Captain Prince were these persons,

and with both of them you are already acquainted. It was not until 1817, when President Monroe visited these Northern States,
that harmony was restored between the two
great divisions, and friends once more em-
braced each other. But, in the midst of all
this excitement with politics, Mr. Bowditch
never neglected the duties of his office, or his
studies. In fact, the pursuit of learning had,
as before, a sweet influence over his character.
It still gave calmness when circumstances
around him tended to disturb him. An illustration of this you may find in what follows.
In 1812, after a long series of supposed insults
and wrongs from Great Britain, the American
government declared war against that power.
Mr. Bowditch was much distressed by the
news, and for two days was so much overcome that he was unable to study. Friends
who knew him had never seen him look so
sad before on any public emergency. He
could speak of nothing but the disasters that
he foresaw war would entail upon his country.
On the morning of the third day he got up, and,

going down into the parlor, said to his wife,
"It won't do for me to continue in this way.
I *will not* think any more about it." Saying
this, he retired again to his books. The difference in his whole manner was very perceptible. He rarely afterwards allowed himself
to be disturbed by the unfortunate state of
affairs. Such should always be the benign
influences of the study of science and of Nature's laws.

Amid all these various engagements, he was
full of sympathy for others. Wherever he
saw he could aid with his counsel, he did so ;
and many widows and orphans have felt the
influence of his charity. This charity showed
itself chiefly in a desire to improve others.
There was scarcely one of those connected
with him in friendship upon whom he did not
devote some time for their instruction. To
one young lady he taught French, and another
studied Italian with him. If a young man
needed funds, he knew upon whom he could
call with a certainty of substantial aid, even
if he had no money of his own to give

away, for throughout life it was one of the remarkable attributes of Mr. Bowditch's character, that he could persuade many to open their hearts to the poor, who, upon other occasions, were deaf to the common feelings of humanity. For one young person of this kind Mr. Bowditch obtained a subscription sufficient to enable him to continue at the university, whereas his young friend would have been unable to do so without assistance. He was always so zealous in these undertakings, that one scarcely felt under any obligations to him. It was his delight to help, and every one saw that his heart was engaged in the cause. His zeal for humanity was at times immoderate, and the following laughable law case occurred in consequence of it. One day he was informed that a little girl, who lived with him, had been run over by some careless driver; and a crowd, which he could perceive at a little distance from him, was a collection of individuals drawn together on her account. He immediately ran forward, and getting to the outside of the circle, began very energetically to make his way into it. In doing so, he pulled one of the bystanders so forcibly, that the individual, as it will appear in the sequel, was offended. Arriving, however, by dint of hard pushing, at the object of his search, he took his little domestic with him, and led her safely home. On the next day he was much surprised at receiving a summons from a justice of the peace, to appear before him, to answer to the charge of assault and battery upon the individual above mentioned. He answered the call and paid his fine of a few dollars; but the judge, who had been notorious for always making both parties suffer, when it was possible for himself to gain thereby, said, on receiving the fine, " But you say that Mr. —— *pushed* you, after you had *pulled* him." " I did, sir." " Very well; then, if you wish to complain of him, I will fine him likewise." The ludicrous nature of the whole action struck Mr. Bowditch so forcibly that he was not unwilling to increase the folly of it. The plaintiff was then fined, and the affair was ended. It is but right to say, that the judge was considered, previously to this, one entirely unfit for the office. Probably no other would have issued a summons on such an occasion, and the plaintiff was not unjustly punished for having called upon such a person to aid him in prosecuting an individual who, in exerting himself to help another, had slightly disarranged the dress of a bystander.

Mr. Bowditch's desire to aid the unfortunate was exhibited on another occasion, when a poor, overladen horse was the object of his commiseration. A truckman had been violently beating the animal, in order to induce him to pull along a very heavy load, which was too large for his strength. Mr. Bowditch had watched the driver for some time, and at length he stepped earnestly forward, and in abrupt and decided tones ordered him to desist. The truckman was much superior to Mr. Bowditch in personal strength, and was, at first, disposed to ridicule the attempt of his inferior to restrain him. Full of indignation, Mr. Bowditch cried out, " If you dare

touch that horse again, and if you do not
immediately go and get another to assist him,
I will appeal to the law, and you will see
which of us two will conquer." The man
yielded, and Mr. Bowditch went home.

The public institutions of the town felt
his influence. The East India Marine Society, of which I have already spoken, improved
very much under his auspices as president.
It had fallen considerably during high political times, and, when he was chosen chief
officer, he instilled such zeal among the
younger members of it, and obtained so many
new members, that it revived; and soon after
his removal to Boston, the splendid hall was
erected, containing the most remarkable collection of East India curiosities, of which I
spoke in Chapter VI.

In the libraries he had always felt very
much interest. You already know what reason he had for being devoted to the Philosophical Library, for from it he drew most of
his knowledge of science. But there was
another, which had been in existence much

longer than this, called the Social Library. The books contained in these two collections were almost wholly distinct in their characters. In one only works of science were to be found, while the other was chiefly devoted to literature. Mr. Bowditch saw that both of them united would be of great service to the community, for it would not merely combine the books, but the energies of the proprietors. Consequently it appears that he, with another of the Philosophical Library proprietors, was chosen a committee for the purpose of providing for a union. This was happily effected (1810), and the Salem Athenæum arose from the combination. The rooms over his office were chosen as the place for their deposit, and for many years he was one of the most active of the trustees.

There was another institution with which he was intimately connected during the whole of the time he lived in Salem. I allude to the church in which his early friend, Rev. Dr. Prince, officiated. He was one of the committee of the parish, and, though never a

member of the church strictly so called, he
was a constant attendant upon the services,
and had great influence in keeping up the harmony and supporting the true interests of the
congregation.

In the performance of his duties as president of the insurance company, he was faithful and prompt in action. He was frequently placed in circumstances which required
great decision of character. At times a
disposition was shown to deceive him; at
others, a richer stockholder would attempt to
gain advantages over a poorer one. I well remember an anecdote in which it is said a purse-
proud rich man tried to browbeat Mr. Bowditch into doing an act which Mr. Bowditch
thought would be unjust to another poorer
one. The nabob pleaded his riches, and
amount of his stock in the office, and intimat-
ed that he would have his way. "No, sir,
you won't. I stand here in this place to see
justice done, and, as long as I am here, I will
defend the weak." He seldom met with difficulties of this kind, for few dared approach

DR. BOWDITCH'S RESIDENCE AT THE TIME OF HIS DEATH.

him with the intention to be unjust or untrue.
Nothing aroused him so much to an almost
lion-like fierceness as any appearance of wick-
edness in the transaction of public business.
He had much wisdom, likewise, in the selec-
tion of risks, so that the office, while under
his control, succeeded admirably and he left it
prosperous.

During his residence in Salem he was often
invited to seats of honor and trust. We have
already mentioned his political course. In
1806, by the agency of Chief Justice Parsons,
then in the corporation of Harvard College,
he was appointed professor of mathematics in
that university. In 1818 he was requested
by President Jefferson, in very flattering
terms, to accept of a similar office in the University of Virginia. In 1820, he was called
upon by the secretary of war of the United
States, to consent to an appointment at the
Public Military School at West Point. All
of these he refused, as not congenial to his
mind. He always declined talking in public.
He would teach all who came to him, but he

9

could not deliver a public course of lectures. His extreme modesty prevented. For it will be remembered that he was as remarkable, from his youth, for his modesty, amounting, in early life, to diffidence, as he was for his other qualities. Moreover, it should be stated that, at times, he had a certain hesitation in his mode of speaking, which probably would have prevented him from addressing easily a public audience.

In 1818, he was urged to take charge of an insurance office in Boston, but he preferred living in his native place.

CHAPTER IX.

From 1803 *to* 1823 — *age,* 30-50.

Papers published by Mr. Bowditch in the Memoirs of the
Academy; account of some of them. — Total eclipse of
the sun in 1806; effect of it. — Anecdote of Chief Justice Parsons. — Meteor that fell over Weston, Ct.; account of its curious appearance; effect of these papers
upon his fame in Europe. — Chosen member of most of
the learned societies of the Old World. — Quits Salem to
become connected with larger institutions in Boston.

IT should be remembered, that, during these
stormy political times, Mr. Bowditch was
chiefly engaged in making his notes on the
great work to which we have already alluded,
La Place's "Mécanique Céleste," and that it
was between the years 1800 and 1820, that is,
during this same time, that he wrote twenty-
three papers, which were published in the
Memoirs of the American Academy of Arts

and Sciences. Of some of these last I will give you an account. Of the others, were I to mention them, you could understand but little. They relate chiefly to observations made upon the moon; the comets of 1807 and 1811; the eclipses of the sun which took place in 1806 and 1811; measurements of the height of the White Mountains, in New Hampshire; observations on the compass; on a pendulum supported by two points; and the correction of some mistakes in one of the books studied first by him in early life, called Newton's "Principia." A few of these papers I will try to explain to you, at least in part. I commence with his observation upon a total eclipse of the sun, which occurred June 16, 1806. I shall quote nearly the words of the observer. "On the day of the eclipse the weather was remarkably fine, scarcely a cloud being visible in any part of the heavens. I made preparations for the observations in the garden adjoining the house in which I reside, near the northern part of Summer Street, in Salem. Having been disappointed in procuring a telescope of a large magnifying power, I was obliged to make use of that attached to my theodolite, which gave very distinct vision, though its magnifying power was small. An assistant was seated near me, who counted the seconds from a chronometer, and thus enabled me to mark down with a pencil, the time when the first impression was made on the sun, without taking my eye from the telescope till four or five seconds had elapsed, and the eclipse had sensibly increased, after which I examined the second and minute hands of the chronometer, and took every precaution to prevent mistakes. Four or five minutes before the commencement of the eclipse, I began to observe that part of the sun where the first contact [of the moon's shadow] was expected to take place; and eight minutes twenty-eight seconds after ten o'clock, I observed the first impression. As the eclipse advanced, there did not appear to be so great a diminution of the light as was generally expected; and it was not till the sun was nearly covered that the darkness was very sensible.

The last ray of light disappeared instantaneously. The moon was then seen surrounded by a luminous appearance of considerable extent, such as has been generally taken notice of in total eclipses of the sun." A number of stars became visible. The observer mentions that the light in the garden was not entirely gone; but in the house candles were needed, as if it were evening. At thirty-two minutes eighteen seconds after eleven o'clock, — that is, at a little more than an hour from the beginning of the eclipse, — the first returning ray of light burst forth with great splendor. I have heard that the effect upon those who saw it was surpassingly grand. Suddenly the light of midday seemed to break in upon the quiet of evening. So completely were all the animal creation deceived, that the cows returned lowing homeward, and the fowls sought their roosts, and quietly placed their heads under their wings. All human beings were looking in mute amazement, and deep silence prevailed, as the dark shadow of the moon came stealing over the surface of the sun at noon.

There was something fearful when the sun was wholly covered. Suddenly a bright ray shot forth mid heaven, and fell upon the earth, and with it arose a loud shout from the assembled crowd. Aged men * and women joined in the chorus, and saluted again the beautiful sunlight.

This paper, though short, is one of the most important he ever wrote. In a note to it he first mentions publicly a mistake he had discovered in the "Mécanique Céleste."

In 1815, Mr. Bowditch published another paper, which I may be able to explain to you in some degree. You have all heard of falling stars, or meteors, and probably most of you have seen them frequently, when walking at night, when the sky is clear. Some of these are very small; they seem at a great distance. They suddenly appear in our heav-

---

* Chief Justice Parsons, it is said, used to say that moment was one of the most exciting of his life; and he could not forbear throwing up his hat and joining in the shout with which the boys saluted the first returning light of the sun.

ens, and as suddenly disappear, and perhaps
nothing more is heard or seen of them.
Others, on the contrary, appear larger, and
fall to the earth after having traversed a great
portion of the heavens. On the 14th of
December, 1807, one of the most curious
exploded, and fell over Weston, in Connecticut. Mr. Bowditch, in his Memoir, writes
thus : —

" The extraordinary meteor which appeared
at Weston, in Connecticut, on the 14th of
December, 1807, and exploded with several
discharges of stones, having excited great
attention throughout the United States, and
being one of those phenomena of which few
exact observations are to be found in the history of physical science, I have thought that a
collection of the best observations of its appearance at different places, with the necessary
deductions for determining, as accurately as
possible, the height, direction, velocity, and
magnitude of the body, would not be unac-
ceptable to the Academy, since facts of this
kind, besides being objects of great curiosity,

may be useful in the investigation of the origin and nature of these meteors; and as the methods of making these calculations are not fully explained in any treatise of trigonometry common in this country, I have given the solutions of two of the most necessary problems, with examples calculated at full length. The second problem is not, to my knowledge, given in any treatise of spherics. The observations of the meteor, which, after many inquiries, were found to have been made with sufficient accuracy to be introduced in the present investigation, were those made at Wenham, about seven miles north-easterly of Salem, by Mrs. Gardner, a very intelligent lady, who had an opportunity of observing it with great attention; those at Weston, by Judge Wheeler and Mr. Staples; and those at Rutland, in Vermont, by William Page, Esq." After giving the requisite solutions, he proceeds: " Some time after the appearance of the meteor, I went with Mr. Pickering to Mrs. Gardner's house, at Wenham, where she had observed the phenomenon. She informed us that on the morning of the 14th of December, 1807, when she arose, she went towards the window of her chamber, which looks to the westward, for the purpose of observing the weather, according to her invariable practice for many years past. The sky was clear, except a few thin clouds in the west. It was past daybreak, and, by estimation, about half an hour before sunrise, or seven o'clock. The meteor was immediately observed just over the southern part of the barn in her farm-yard, nearly in front of the window; its disk was well defined, and it resembled the moon so much, that, unprepared as Mrs. G.'s mind was for a phenomenon of that nature, she was not at first aware that it was not the moon, till she perceived it in motion, when her first thought (to use her own words) was, 'Where is the moon going to?' The reflection, however, was hardly made, when she corrected herself, and with her eye followed the body with the closest attention throughout its whole course. It moved in a direction nearly parallel to the horizon, and disappeared behind a cloud northward of the house of Samuel Blanchard, Esq. She supposed the meteor to have been visible about half a minute.

" The attention of Judge Wheeler was first drawn by a sudden flash of light, which illuminated every object. Looking up, he discovered, in the north, a globe of fire just then passing behind the cloud which obscured, though it did not entirely hide, the meteor. In this situation its appearance was distinct and well defined, like that of the sun seen through a mist. It rose from the north, and proceeded in a direction nearly perpendicular to the horizon, but inclining by a very small angle to the west, and deviating a little from the plane of a great circle, but in pretty large curves, sometimes on one side of the plane and sometimes on the other, but never making an angle with it of more than four or five degrees. Its apparent diameter was about one half or two thirds the apparent diameter of the full moon. Its progress was not so rapid as that of common meteors and shooting stars. When it passed behind the thinner clouds, it appeared brighter than before; and when it passed the spots of clear sky, it flashed with a vivid light, yet not so intense as the lightning of a thunder-storm. Where it was not too much obscured by thick clouds, a waving, conical train of paler light was seen to attend it, in length about ten or twelve diameters of the body. In the clear sky a brisk scintillation was observed about the body of the meteor, like that of a burning firebrand carried against the wind. It disappeared about fifteen degrees short of the zenith, and about the same number of degrees west of the meridian. It did not vanish instantaneously, but grew, pretty rapidly, fainter and fainter, as a red-hot cannon-ball would do if cooling in the dark, only with much more rapidity. The whole period between its first appearance and total extinction was estimated at about thirty seconds. About thirty or forty seconds after this, three loud and distinct reports, like those of a four-pounder near at hand, were heard. Then followed a rapid succession of reports less loud, so as to produce a continued rumbling. This noise continued about as long as the body was in rising, and died away, apparently, in the direction from which the meteor came. Mr. Staples observed that when the meteor disappeared, there were apparently three successive efforts or leaps of the fire-ball, which grew more dim at every throe, and disappeared with the last. From the various accounts which we have received of the appearance of the body, at different places, we are inclined to believe that the time between the disappearance and report, as estimated by Judge Wheeler, is too little, and that a minute is the least time that could have intervened.

" The observations made at Rutland were procured by the kind offices of Professor Hall, of Middlebury College, Vermont, to whom Mr. Page communicated his valuable observations, in a paper expressed in the following terms : ' I was at the west door of my house, on Monday morning, the 14th of December, 1807, about daylight ; and perceiving the sky suddenly illuminated, I raised my eyes and beheld a meteor of a circular form, in the south-westerly part of the heavens, rapidly descending to the south, leaving behind it a vivid, sparkling train of light. The atmosphere near the south part of the horizon was very hazy; but the passage of the meteor behind the clouds was visible until it descended below the mountains, about twenty miles south of this place. There were white, fleecy clouds scattered about the sky, but none so dense as to obscure the track of the meteor. I now lament that I did not make more particular observations at the time; and I should probably, until this day, have considered it to be what is commonly called a " falling star," had I not read in the New York papers an account of the explosion of a meteor, and the falling of some meteoric stones near New Haven, Connecticut, which, by recurring to circumstances then fresh in my recollection, I found to be on the same morning that I observed the meteor at Rutland. I am indebted to my learned friend Dr. Samuel Williams for his aid and directions in ascertaining the situation of the meteor when I first observed it, and its course, and also for the order of my observations : Form, circular ; magnitude, less than a quarter of the diameter of the moon ; color, red, vivid light ; tail, or train of light, about eight times the length of its diameter, at the least, projected opposite to its course.' "

I quote these to give you some idea of the appearance of this meteor, and likewise of Mr. Bowditch's diligence. From the examination of all the accounts given him, he came to the conclusion that the body moved at the rate of more than three miles per second, and at the height of eighteen miles above the surface of the earth. With regard to the magnitude of the body, the results were less accurate ; and the probability is, that all the body did not fall, but merely passed through the air, and continued on its course into unknown regions of space.*

* Since the first edition of this memoir, the whole subject of meteoric stones has been more thoroughly investigated by astronomers. Professor Loomis, of New Haven,

The other papers I shall not mention, because they are upon subjects difficult to be comprehended.   The last appeared in the volumes of the Memoirs of the Academy published in 1820.   All these papers were read by the astronomers and mathematicians of Europe, and the consequence was, that Mr. Bowditch was chosen a member of many of the learned societies instituted there for the promotion of science.   In 1818 he was chosen into the Royal Societies of London and Edinburgh, and in the year following was enrolled on the list of the Royal Irish Academy.   While

says (Elements of Astronomy, 1869, page 209), "In the year 1833, shooting stars appeared in extraordinary numbers, on the morning of November 14.   It was estimated that they fell at the rate of five hundred and seventy-five per minute.   Most of these meteors moved in paths, which, if traced backward, would meet in a point near Gamma, in the constellation Leo.   A similar exhibition took place on the 12th of November, 1799, and there are recorded ten other similar appearances at about the same period of the year.

"There was a repetition of this remarkable display of meteors on the morning of November 14, 1866, when the number amounted to one hundred and twenty-six per min-

I am upon this subject, I would state that he afterwards was elected associate of the Astronomical Society of London, of the Academies of Berlin and Palermo, and had a correspondence with most of the astronomers of Europe. The National Institute of France was about choosing him one of its candidates for the position of foreign member, only eight of which are chosen from the whole world. He died before any election was held.

In addition to the papers to the Academy, Mr. Bowditch published several articles in reviews, &c. One of them is an interest-

ute; also November 14, 1867, when the number of meteors for a short time amounted to two hundred and twenty per minute; and November 14, 1868, the display was about equally remarkable."

Professor Loomis concludes that "these meteors belong to a system of bodies describing an elliptic orbit about the sun, and making a revolution in thirty-three years."

The Weston meteor, or aerolite, observed by Dr. Bowditch, is mentioned by Professor Loomis, as one of "great brilliancy." "The entire weight of the fragments discovered was at least three hundred pounds. . . . The length of the visible path of this meteor exceeded one hundred miles. It moved about fifteen miles per second."

10

ing history of modern astronomy, which is
intended to give us an account of the lives
and doings of the most celebrated astronomers of modern times. Such were his principal literary labors, and the greater part of
them were performed during his residence in
Salem.

The article on modern astronomy was prepared a few years after his removal to Boston.
To that removal let us now turn. In 1823
overtures were made to him to control two
institutions in Boston, one for life insurance,
the other for marine risks. The offers were
too liberal for him to refuse. His duties to
his family compelled him to accept them. On
his determination being known, his fellow-
citizens paid him a pleasant tribute of respect
and love by inviting him to a public and
farewell dinner.

As the family left Salem, Mr. Bowditch and
his wife often thought that, after remaining
eight or ten years at Boston, they would return, in order that their bodies might be laid
by the side of those of their ancestors. But

new friends awaited them in Boston; new ties were formed there; and although they always looked to their native place as the seat of many of their most beloved associations, they both lived in Boston until their deaths.

His engagements of a public nature, during his residence in Boston, were similar to those he had whilst at Salem. For many years he managed both of the institutions to which he had been called. But the directors, finding that the duties of one were sufficient to occupy all his attention, broke up the Marine Insurance Company, and Mr. Bowditch (or Dr. Bowditch, as he was now generally called, having received the degree of Doctor of Laws from Harvard University in 1816) devoted himself to the life insurance office. This he raised to be one of the greatest institutions in New England. By an alteration in the charter, proposed by Dr. Bowditch, this became, in fact, a great savings bank, where immense sums are now yearly put in trust for widows and orphans. The only difference in his habits, caused by his removal to Boston, was an enlargement of his sphere of labor. All objects of public utility still engaged his attention.

The system of popular lectures, of which we have now so many, commenced with the Mechanic Institution of which he was the first president.   He was zealous for the improvement of the Boston Athenæum, and was very influential towards getting for it large sums of money, and in making it more liberal in its rules.

An honor was conferred upon him, after his arrival in Boston, which he thought as high as any ever received.   Having had two honorary degrees from Harvard University, and having been one of the board of overseers of that institution for many years, he was finally chosen a member of the corporation, or council of seven men, who guide the whole of the concerns of that important institution.   How different the commencement and termination of the career of the poor son of a cooper, who at ten years of age left school, and yet at the end of life was one of the chief directors in the first literary institution in America !

CHAPTER X.

Sketch of the life of La Place, author of the "Mécanique Céleste." — Newton's labors. — Halley's comet. — The importance of astronomy to navigation. — Comets; Dr. Bowditch translates the Mécanique Céleste; difficulties attending the undertaking; objects he had in view; first volume analyzed; Newton's error pointed out.

In a former part of this story of Dr. Bowditch's life, you will remember that I stated that on his last voyage he commenced his notes upon the "Mécanique Céleste" of La Place. It was on the first day of November, during his disagreeable voyage homewards, in 1803, that he wrote his first note to the work which was destined to occupy much of his time from that moment until his death, thirty-five years afterwards, in Boston. This work certainly deserves some of our attention, if he thought it worthy of receiving the attention of so many years of his life. A brief account of the life of the author of the original work may interest you, and will serve as an introduction to the book itself.

Pierre Simon La Place was born on the 23d of March, in the year 1749, at Beaumont, on the borders of the beautiful and fertile country of ancient Normandy, situated in the north-western part of France. He was the son of simple peasants in that country, and from his earliest years was remarkable for the extraordinary powers of memory, and intense love of study, with which he was endowed. In early life every branch of learning was delightful to him. He seemed eager to gain knowledge merely, without regard to the object of his study. But he soon began to distinguish himself upon the subject of theology. This pursuit, however, was soon ended, and by some means, of which no details now remain, his mind was led to mathematics, and from that moment he was devoted to them. After spending his youth at his native place, and having taught mathematics

there, he, at the age of eighteen years, went
to Paris, to seek a wider sphere in his pursuit of knowledge.   Bearing several letters
of recommendation as a youth of great promise, he presented himself at the abode of
D'Alembert, who at that time was the first
mathematician of France, and contended with
Euler, at Berlin, for the honor of being the
first in the world.   But the letters upon which
the youth depended so much proved of no
use.   D'Alembert passed them by in silent
neglect, without even deigning to receive at
his own house the bearer of them.   But La
Place was fully bent upon success, and relying
upon the force of his own genius as a more powerful recommendation than any letters, he sent
to D'Alembert an essay, written by himself,
upon a very abstruse subject relating to mechanics.   The professor, struck with its elegance
and the great learning displayed by it, soon afterwards called upon the writer, and addressed
him in these words : "You see, sir, that I think
recommendations are worth but very little ;
and for yourself they are wholly unnecessary.

By your own writings you can make yourself
better known than by any other means. They
are sufficient. I will do all I can for you."
In a few days after this conversation, the
young man was appointed professor of mathematics in the public military school at Paris.
From this period until the end of his life he.
was occupied upon the science which he was
thus called, at this early age, to teach publicly
at the capital of France. He became daily
more acquainted with the great men of the
nation, and was himself making additions to
the scientific acquirements of the age, thus
giving eminent proofs of his genius. He was
chosen member of the French Academy, a
society of learned men united for the purpose of advancing the cause of learning, and
he stood soon very high amongst them.

His chief work, the " Celestial Mechanics,"
— " *Mécanique Céleste*,"— he began to publish
in 1799, and finished the fourth volume in
1805.* This placed him much above all his

---

* A fifth was printed several years afterwards, on which
Mr. Bowditch made some notes, and which he meant to
have published, but death prevented him from so doing.

contemporaries. In it he had not only combined many things which he himself had discovered, but likewise gave a history, as it were, of all that had been done by geometricians from the time of Sir Isaac Newton until his own day. La Place found many things detached, but his genius proved that many apparently discordant facts could be explained by Newton's theory of universal gravitation. His labor must have been immense. All Europe rang with the fame of this production, which was said to be beyond anything ever performed before by man. The echo of its fame reached America, and Dr. Bowditch obtained the volumes, as they were successively published. The first two he received in part payment for his labors on the "Navigator."

Soon after his arrival home from his fourth voyage, Dr. Bowditch was taking his accustomed walk towards the lower part of the town of Salem, and met his old friend, Captain Prince. They entered into conversation, and Dr. Bowditch remarked that he had, a short time before, received a book from France, which he had long wished for, having heard that it was superior to anything ever before written by man, and which very few were able to comprehend. This work was that to which I have been alluding, and it now renders Dr. Bowditch's own name familiarly known among mathematicians.

Later in life, La Place published a work called the " System of the World." In this, which, comparatively speaking, is not difficult to be read by almost any one, he attempts to give a plain and simple statement of all that is known in regard to those wise and magnificent laws, whereby this solar system is kept together in perfect harmony, while at the same time it is sailing onward through fields of space.

La Place, however, was not a truly noble man, because he was not strictly just. It is said that he was willing to attribute to himself the discoveries of others. On Napoleon Bonaparte's becoming first consul in France, La Place was made one of the ministers of the state; but he was soon found to be better fit-

ted for study than for the practical duties of
a public office. Accordingly he retired after a
few weeks' service, but was made a member
of the Senate, of which he became president.
After finishing his political career, he published other works of great moment; but of
those I shall not speak. About the year 1827
he was seized with an acute disorder, which
soon terminated his life. His last words are
remarkable, as conveying the same truth that
every wise man has upon his lips at the hour
of death. As he reviewed the amount of his
learning, which was in one respect greater
than that of any man living, he exclaimed,
" What we know here is very little, but what
we are ignorant of is immense." Every man
is compelled to become silent and modest as
he sees death approach. La Place was like
other common men. He died as a man, and
was buried, and the men of science felt sad
that one so learned and of so strong an intellect should have departed. Endowed by the
Almighty with the loftiest powers of intellect,
he stood alone, and commanded the respect, if

he did not always gain the love, of his associ-
ates. Dr. Bowditch, though he regarded La
Place as the greatest mathematician that had
ever lived, had little real sympathy with his
character.

We must now try to give you a short account of the " Mécanique Céleste," and of Dr.
Bowditch's labors upon it. The original work
consists of five volumes, but Dr. Bowditch
lived to finish the translation of and commentary upon only the first four. There are
about fifteen hundred pages in the original,
while there are three thousand eight hundred
and eighteen in the American translation.
The object of the original work may be known
from the following introductory remarks by
La Place, on the occasion of printing the first
volume, in 1798 : " Newton, towards the end
of the last century, published his discovery
of the laws of gravity, or of the power by
which the solar system is held together.
Since that period, geometricians have succeeded in bringing under this law all the known
phenomena of the system of the universe. I

mean to bring together those scattered themes
and facts upon this subject, so as to form one
whole, which shall embrace all the known results of gravity upon the motions, forms, &c.,
of the fluid and solid bodies that compose our
solar system, as well as of those other similar
systems that are spread around in the immen-
sity of space." You probably all understand
from this quotation the general object of the
" Mécanique Céleste." La Place likewise in-
forms us that the work is divided into two
parts. In the first he proposes to give' the
methods for determining the motions of the
heavenly bodies, their forms, the motions of
the oceans and seas upon their surfaces, and
finally the movements of rotation of these
spheres about their own axes. In the second
part, he promises to apply the rules which he
has given in the first to the planets and the
satellites which move around them, and
likewise to the comets. The first part is
found in the first two volumes, the second
part occupies the last two. From these few
remarks you will perceive the immense task

imposed upon himself by La Place, and at
the same time the grandeur of it. How wonderful, that a simple man can attempt to mark
out the course of the heavenly bodies, which
we see clustering around us at night! But
how much more wonderful does man become,
when we find he has the *power* to foretell to
us the return of comets that have never been
seen by any one living now — comets that
have been, during our lives, travelling into
the far-off fields of space! Strange that a
simple man can prophesy, to a day, their return! Many of us now living remember a
beautifully bright and clear comet, which
in 1835 appeared, as had been predicted,
after an absence of seventy-six years. It was
called Halley's comet, after its first discoverer.
At first it seemed like a bright speck in the
heavens towards the north; but the next night
it was larger. It seemed to approach, with
fearful rapidity, from evening to evening,
and, sweeping in majesty across our western
sky, disappeared gradually in its progress
towards the sun, around which it whirled,

and again appeared, more faintly visible than
before, just over our eastern horizon, as if to
give us one more glimpse of itself, a strange
messenger of the Almighty, before it passed
off on its far-distant journey, not to return
until those who were then young and free as air,
are all laid quietly in the grave, or have become enfeebled and decrepit by the approach
of age. Truly, great is God, who made the
comet; but to me man also seems full of
grandeur, when I find him capable of even
foretelling the exact passage of such a body.
Yet La Place enables any man to prophesy
this; and in his "Mécanique Céleste" we
may find all the methods of investigation necessary for this object. But he likewise tells
us the forms of the planets; he enables us to
measure the ring which surrounds the planet
Saturn, and enables us to decide, at least in
some degree the form and mass of the sun. In
this same work he treats of those curious phenomena, which, as we see them daily, we think
of little moment — the flow and ebb of the sea,
or, in other words, high and low tides, — and

the causes of them. He treats of the motion of
the earth about its centre, and of the same motions in the moon and planets. These are the
chief objects of the first and second volumes.
The third volume, as we have already hinted,
contains questions of great intricacy, and of immense importance; namely, the exact motions
of the planets around the sun, as affected by all
the attractions exerted upon them by the various
bodies of the universe; and the still more important motions of our moon around the earth.
I say important, because the exact knowledge
of the course of this body is of the greatest moment to every sailor who attempts to go from
one country to another over the trackless ocean.
By means of observations upon this planet,
the seaman can sail over distant waters for
many months, and be able to return, when he
may wish, to his own home in safety. Hence
the importance of the astronomer to the simple navigator of our planet. The history of
Dr. Bowditch is another proof of the truth of
this statement. By his accurate knowledge
of astronomy, by his ability to follow La

Place in his investigations of all the motions of the solar system, he was enabled to produce a work on navigation which is sought for wherever the English language is spoken, as it combines the best methods of using the results of pure astronomy in the art of navigation. The "Practical Navigator" would never have maintained its hold upon the community as it has done, if Dr. Bowditch had not been as skilful in mathematics and astronomy as in the details of navigation.

But to return to the "Mécanique Céleste." The fourth volume contains similar investigations, namely, the motions of the satellites, or moons, about the other planets. Our moon's motions about the earth, and the revolutions of Jupiter's satellites are the most important. Jupiter has four satellites. These were the first that the invention of the telescope by Galileo revealed to man; and by their frequent revolutions around the planet, they have in their turn shown to us many of the laws which govern the whole planetary system, besides many curious and interesting facts in regard to their own

11

forms and masses. From the eclipses or disappearances of the first satellite, when it passes on the side of the planet opposite to that at which the observer from the earth is looking, it has demonstrated the velocity of light. Finally, the author treats of the seven moons, or satellites, of Saturn, and likewise of those of the planet Herschel, about which much less is known.*

After attending to these subjects, La Place investigates the powers which act upon comets, which tend to turn from their courses those bodies, which, as I have before said, are

---

* Since the first edition of this memoir, one of the most extraordinary results ever obtained in astronomy by the use of these same methods of investigation has been made known. Messrs. Leverrier, a French astronomer, and Adams of England, calculated very exactly the general characteristics and course of a planet, which, from the disturbances of the courses of other well-known planets, was *supposed* to exist. In 1846, Leverrier requested a German astronomer to point his telescope, at a certain time, towards a certain part of the heavens, and there was the long-suspected planet, previously never seen! It was named Neptune. It is sixty times larger than our earth, and its orbit is nearly thirty times farther distant from the sun.

flying in very many directions throughout the universe, and which are liable to be moved out of their direction by the actions of some planets near which they may come. This was the case with a comet in 1770, whose course was wholly changed by the planet Jupiter drawing it towards its own body. To investigate the various laws of these disturbing forces is one subject of this volume. Some other subjects are treated of, but of these I shall now not speak.

From this brief account of the "Mécanique Céleste" you may judge of the difficulties which the original writer had to overcome in making it, and of the immense labor requisite. But La Place frequently supposes that a proposition is perfectly intelligible to his reader because it is so to him. Having such a powerful mind, he is able to see at a glance that for which any one else would require a long demonstration, before he could become thoroughly master of the subject. The consequence of this is, an obscurity in the work, which has made it doubly difficult of comprehension. Several years ago, but a long time

after Dr. Bowditch had read and made notes
upon the whole work, an English writer said
that there were scarcely twelve men in Europe
capable of comprehending it.   Dr. Bowditch,
feeling that it was the most valuable work
upon astronomy published in modern times,
had undertaken the translation of it, and had
made notes thereupon, for the purpose of
" amusing his leisure hours."   Upon its being
known that he had finished the task, the
American Academy offered to publish it.   Dr.
Bowditch would not allow this, and reserved
the publication until he was able to do so at
his own expense.   Let us see, now, what service Dr. Bowditch intended to perform by his
translation and commentary.   His first object
was to lay before America the greatest work
on the science of astronomy ever published.
Secondly, his aim was to bring that work
down to the comprehension of young men, and
students of mathematics, by filling up those
places left by La Place without demonstration.
Thirdly, he meant to give the history of the
science of astronomy for the interval between
the publication of the original work and that

at which the translation appeared. Fourthly, he wished to collect together all the discoveries which he had made during the forty years of his life that he had devoted to science. His first aim was gained by the translation. His second was completely successful, for he was assured by correspondents, both in America and Europe, that he had enabled several to read the immortal work of La Place, who never would have done so had not Dr. Bowditch published his Commentary. The royal astronomer at Palermo says, in a printed work published after the first two volumes of the translation had reached him, " Bowditch's Commentary should be translated into Italian ; " and Lacroix, a celebrated French mathematician, advised a young Swiss to read La Place in the American edition rather than in the original. But what pleased the commentator more than anything else, were the frequent letters from young men residing in various parts of America, expressing gratitude for the benefits they had received from his work. When I think of these, I am reminded of the epithet bestowed upon Dr. Bowditch since his death, and by one well capable of judging, namely, "Father of American Mathematics." He has given a tone to the study of science which will be long felt.

In regard to the third object, all critics allow that he was eminently successful in giving the history of science up to the time proposed.

Upon the fourth point, we might refer, first, to the immense increase of bulk of the work, as a proof, but I prefer to mention a few details; and in order to this, let us examine the Commentary, and let it speak for itself. But it must be remembered, that, in making this examination, I must omit many circumstances, because you would not understand or feel interested in any greater detail.

In the first volume he points out two errors of La Place, one of which relates to the motion of the earth; and the other is of much importance. It relates to the permanency of our solar system, as it is commonly called. You all doubtless know that the sun is situated in the centre, and the planets, with our earth, revolve around this luminary, which gives light and heat to all. Now, these bodies revolve in certain fixed " nearly circular " directions, and La Place thought that they would always continue to do so, and that Mercury, Venus, the Earth, Mars, Jupiter, Saturn, and Herschel would forever continue to wheel around in their accustomed orbits. Dr. Bowditch proves, however, that though this may be true of the three larger planets, — Jupiter, Saturn, and Herschel, — it is not equally certain, *from the proofs given by La Place,* that our earth, or any of the other smaller planets, may not fly off into regions far remote from those in which they have been revolving for ages. This error had been made the subject of a paper to the American Academy at an earlier period of his life. But it must not be supposed that there is any proof that the solar system will not continue to exist for many long ages. On the contrary, there is no doubt that it will last millions of years. Dr. Bowditch merely wished to assert that La Place's argument and calculation did not prove as much as the French mathematician thought they did. In this volume Dr.

Bowditch likewise alludes to a topic which he had made the subject of a communication, a long time previously, to the American Academy; I refer to a mistake in Newton's "Principia," which he discovered when quite young, and had sent an account of to the president of Harvard College. This gentleman referred the question to the professor of mathematics, who believed the youth was mistaken. Doubtless he thought it very strange that a simple youth should presume to correct anything published by so eminent a man as Newton. The error of the professor will become less singular when you learn that the same mistake escaped the notice of all the commentators on the "Principia," — that is, for more than a century, — and that the cause of the original communication being made to the Academy was the attempt of Mr. Emerson, an Englishman, to prove the correctness of the English philosopher. Every one, I believe, now allows that Dr. Bowditch was correct, and that a considerable error would result, in calculating the orbit of a comet, from using Newton's calculations.

CHAPTER XI.

Commentary continued; second volume. — Discussion between the English and French mathematicians; Dr. Bowditch's criticisms. — Errors in La Place in regard to the earth, &c. — Third volume; motions of the moon. — Fourth volume; many errors discovered in it. — Halley's Comet. — Curious phenomena of capillary attraction.

In the second volume of the Commentary, Dr. Bowditch makes very copious notes, in which he shows a perfect knowledge of the works of the chief mathematicians of Europe. He stands as critic between two of the eminent men of science of that day — Messrs. Ivory and Poisson, the former an Englishman, the latter a Frenchman; and in reference, likewise, to a difficult subject, namely, the revolution or the turning of a fluid mass upon its own axis, as our earth does. He not merely agrees with Mr. Poisson, but, by a very simple illustration, proves the total inaccuracy of Mr. Ivory's views. I well remember the earnestness with which he studied this subject. Day after day, he returned to the task of finding out some " simple case," with which to prove to the satisfaction of others the truth of his own view. At length, when he did discover it, he jumped up in ecstasy, and, rubbing his hands and forehead with delight, walked about the library-room, crying out, "I have got it!"

Dr. Bowditch in this volume points out five errors or omissions made by La Place, some of which are very important. One refers to the form of our earth, and had been previously communicated to the Academy. There is another of some moment, relative to the time occupied in the revolution of one of Saturn's rings, La Place having made it longer than was true.

Finally, on the subject of the motion of the earth about its centre of gravity, he points out an error, in which La Place gives to two numbers only one third of their true value.

In the third volume, occupied as it is with the motions of the planets and of the moon, and with all the phenomena accompanying these, Dr. Bowditch shows much learning, and his power of bringing modern science to the thorough study of any topic. As in the previous volume, he labors without fear upon subjects treated of with much earnestness by La Place, Poisson, and Pontecoulant, in France, and Plana in Italy.

On the theory of the motions of the moon, — a very difficult and interesting subject, — Dr. Bowditch makes very copious notes; and the volume terminates with an appendix of more than two hundred and fifty pages, in which he gives the history of modern astronomy, in reference to the calculations of the movements of planets and comets. In this he speaks of Olbers and Gauss. The former, from having discovered three planets since the beginning of this century, was called "The fortunate Columbus of the Heavens." The latter was one of the most remarkable men in the world for the rapidity with which he was able to perform the most tedious and troublesome calculations.*

We come now to the last volume, in printing the thousandth page of which he died. It was the most difficult to him of the whole, and probably will raise him higher, in the estimation of the scientific world, than either of the others. In the first place, I would remark, that either from the difficulty of the subject, or from the inattention of La Place, an unusual number of errors was discovered. No less than twenty-four errors or omissions are pointed out. Many of these seem insignificant, but often, as may be supposed, they materially affect the calculation. Most of them refer to the derangements and the motions of Jupiter's satellites — a subject which occupies three hundred and fourteen pages of the volume. The keenness of Dr. Bowditch's criticism is again perceived while treating

---

* Within the last few years numerous other smaller bodies (asteroids) have been discovered — not less than eighty being now known.

upon a subject in dispute between Plana and La Place. Dr. Bowditch points out one mistake, and Poisson another, whereby Plana's views are proved to coincide entirely with La Place's, instead of being opposed to them.

I find a note upon Halley's comet, to which I alluded as presenting a grand spectacle in our western sky a few years since, and I cannot forbear mentioning the coincidence. Dr. Bowditch, when making his notes upon the subject of the motions and revolutions of comets, speaks of Halley's comet, and mentions all that is known about it, and its probable appearance. This note was prepared some time before it was printed. It terminates thus : "Since writing the preceding part of this note the comet has again appeared, and, *at the time of printing this page, is visible in the heavens*, not far distant from the place corresponding to the elements of Mr. Pontecoulant."

The work, so far as Dr. Bowditch is concerned, finishes with the most curious and difficult subject of capillary attraction, or that

power whereby a liquid rises in narrow tubes
beyond the level of the fluid outside, as we
see familiarly in sponges, and cloths, and in
very minute glass tubes. You may think this
subject of little moment; yet La Place
thought it more curious than almost any other, and he earnestly calls the attention of
mathematicians to it. It is a subject so difficult of investigation, that it requires the
keenest efforts of the best intellects to rightly
understand it. After La Place's investigations
were published, Gauss considered the subject,
and arrived at results similar to those presented by La Place. But in 1831, Poisson,
the first mathematician then living, of whom
we have already spoken, put forth a work in
which he announced many new views. This
he thought himself justified in doing, after taking into consideration certain particulars which
La Place had neglected. Dr. Bowditch received the work while engaged in printing this
volume. He ceased printing, and devoted six
months or more to a thorough perusal of the
new French work. The result was, that he

proved that without an exception, unless where an evident error was made by La Place, the principles of this mathematician, when fairly carried out, would produce all the results which Poisson had given as new in his work. By this labor Dr. Bowditch proved that Poisson's so-called new theory of capillary attraction was founded in error. This is decidedly the most important work of the translator. It places him much higher than before in the scale of mathematical rank.

I would willingly give a further analysis, but I forbear, because it would not be interesting to you. It was in correcting this, his noblest task, in the full strength of his intellect, that he was destined to die.

CHAPTER XII.

Sketch of the life of La Grange, the equal of La Place;
love Dr. Bowditch had for this person's character; comparison between him and La Place; also between him
and Dr. Bowditch. — Conclusion of the Memoir.

DURING this history I frequently have
spoken of different individuals; but there is
one about whom little mention has been made,
but of whose life I wish to give you a short
account, as his character resembles very much
that of Dr. Bowditch. His mind and heart
were always regarded by the American mathematician with feelings of respect and love,
such as he felt towards no other mathematician
whose works he had studied. An equal of
La Place, it seems not improper to mention
him; and I know you will excuse the slight
interruption in my story when you perceive
how the noble nature of La Grange seems to

harmonize with, and to illustrate, as it were, the life of Dr. Bowditch.

Joseph Louis La Grange, one of the most famous geometricians of modern times, was born at Turin, January 25, 1736. He was one of eleven children of parents who became very poor, so that Joseph had in early life to gain his own subsistence. When young, he devoted himself to the classics, and read Latin constantly. At seventeen his taste for abstruse mathematics and geometry first showed itself; and from this period he continued studying by himself, without aid. In two years he had acquired a knowledge of all that was known upon the science, and began to correspond with the scientific men of other lands. In 1755 he sent to Euler, then the greatest mathematician in the world, and residing in Berlin, an answer to a problem proposed by Euler, ten years before, to the learned men of Europe, and which they had been unable to solve. He was appointed professor of mathematics at Turin, at the age of nineteen years, and soon afterwards originated

12

the Academy of Sciences at that place. In
their Memoirs he published papers in which he
not merely criticised Euler and D'Alembert
and others, but brought forward some very
curious new views of science, discovered by
himself. Europe soon resounded with his
praises, and he was chosen member of all the
learned societies. In 1766, he was called to
the court of Frederick the Great, King of
Prussia, to take the place of Euler, who was
summoned by the Emperor of Russia to St.
Petersburg. Frederick wrote to him thus:
" Come to my court, for it is right that the
greatest mathematician in Europe should be
near the greatest king." He accepted the situation thus offered, and remained there until
Frederick died; and soon afterwards he was
invited by the French government to go to
Paris. From this time, with slight interrup-
tions, his fame continued to increase, and
every one delighted to honor him; for his labors did honor to his adopted country. One
of the most beautiful compliments, perhaps,
ever paid to man, was the message sent by the

French government to the old father of La
Grange at Piedmont, when that country fell, by
a revolution, under French influence. " Go,"
said the Minister of Foreign Affairs to his am-
bassador, " go to the venerable father of the illustrious La Grange, and say to him, that,
after the events that have just taken place, the
French government look to him as the first object of their interest."   The answer of the old
man was touching : " This day is the happiest
of my life, and my son is the cause of it ! " And
thrice blessed must be such a son, for he fills
the last hours of his father's life with peace.
When Bonaparte came into power, new honors
were showered upon him.   But what was it
that charmed Dr. Bowditch in the character
of La Grange?   It was the combination of a
giant intellect with extreme modesty and simplicity, a sincere love of truth, and almost
feminine affections.   He was a pure being,
whose intellect equalled La Place's, but who
at the same time was full of the utmost gentleness and strict justice.   He was at Berlin
during the earlier part of La Place's career in

Paris. In after-life, the two were friends.
Both were great geniuses; both were capable
of the highest flights of thought, and of bringing down to the comprehension of mankind the
vast and wise laws impressed by God on the
system of the universe. La Place became interested in political life. La Grange stood aside,
quiet and pleased with his own high thoughts.
If his fellows wished him to take upon himself any public duties, he took them cheerfully, and as cheerfully resigned them. La
Place courted honors; La Grange meekly received them. La Place sometimes assumed
the fruits of other men's labors to cover
himself with their glory. In the heart of La
Grange sat humility, justice, and philanthropic
love. In fact, La Grange was full of the
loftiest qualities and genius combined. La
Place had the latter. His genius alone rec-
ommended him to the scientific men around
him. Such were two men whose works Dr.
Bowditch read with the greatest pleasure.
He often spoke with great feeling of the noble
traits in the character of La Grange. The

features and form of the head of Dr. Bowditch resembled those of the great Italian.   I
have often thought that, as they were like
each other in countenance, so their disposi-
tions and fortunes in life were more nearly
similar than is usual in this world.   Both were
born poor, and early had to seek subsistence
for themselves.   Each devoted himself early
to the science of mathematics, and both became eminent in it.   Love of truth and a
longing for it were strong traits in both ; order and regularity of life, and simplicity of
food and regimen, belonged to them equally.
Above all, a sincere reverence for goodness,
for true modesty and delicate refinement, and
a fine respect for the female sex, were strik-
ingly manifest in both.   Both were moderate
in their desires, and both had the highest good
of humanity at heart.   Each sought for quiet
and retirement from the turmoil of life in his
"peaceful mathematics."   As the lives of both
were beautiful, so was the serenity of their
death scenes.   La Grange was attacked near
the end of March, 1813, by a severe fever,

and the symptoms soon became alarming. He saw the danger he was in, but still preserved his serenity. "I am studying," says he, " what is passing within me, as if I were now engaged in some great and rare experiment." On the 8th of April, his friends Messrs. Lacépède, Monge, and Chaptal visited him, and in a long conversation which he entered into with them, he showed that his memory was still unclouded, and his intellect as bright as ever. He spoke to them of his actual condition, of his labors, of his success, of the tenor of his life, and expressed no regret at dying, except at the idea of being separated from his wife, whose kind attentions had been unremittingly bestowed upon him. He soon sank and died. Three days afterwards his body was deposited in the Pantheon, as it is called, the burial-place for the great men of France; and La Place and his friend Lacépède delivered their tributes of praise and admiration over his grave. So peaceful and calm was the death of Dr. Bowditch, whose life I have been trying to place before you.

Dr. Bowditch's health had been generally good, though he never was robust. In 1808 he was dangerously ill with a cough, and by the advice of a physician, he took a journey in an open chaise. He was driven towards Pawtucket and Providence, thence in a westerly direction through Hartford and New Haven to Albany, and back again across the interior of Massachusetts, as far as the fertile valley of the Connecticut River. Thence passing upwards, he crossed on the southern borders of Vermont and New Hampshire to Newburyport, and back to Salem. This journey restored him, and he never afterwards suffered much from cough, and generally enjoyed good health until his last illness.

In 1834 his wife died. His heart was borne down by the loss. She had been to him always a loving and a tender companion, faithful and true even to the minutest points. She had watched all his labors. She had urged him onward in the pursuit of science, by telling him that she would find the means of meeting any expense by her own economy in her care of

the family. She had watched the progress of
his greatest work, which, with his dying hands,
he afterwards dedicated to her memory. She
had listened with delight to all the praises
that had come to him from his own countrymen and from foreign lands; and now, when
he was full of honor and yet active in business, she was called to leave him. With her
the real charm of life departed, and many sad
hours would have been the consequence, if his
sense of duty and devotion to science had not
prevented them. He attended now more closely to active engagements. He always spoke of
his wife with extreme fondness, and sometimes
his tears would flow in spite, apparently, of his
efforts to restrain them. There was a degree
of sadness, however, which was perceptible
only to his family, that settled upon Dr. Bowditch during the last four years of life, in
consequence of this deprivation.

In the latter part of the summer and early
days of autumn of 1837, he began to feel that
he was losing strength, and had occasionally
pains of great severity. He continued to

attend to the duties of his office, however, without yielding to his suffering. In January, 1838, he submitted to medical advice; but it was of no avail. He sank rapidly under a severe and torturing disease, which, for the last fortnight of life, deprived him of the power of eating or even of drinking anything, except a small quantity of wine and water. Until the last moment of his life, he was engaged in attending to the duties of the Life Office, and to the publication of his Commentary on the "Mécanique Céleste." During this time, after he lost the power of visiting State Street, he used to walk into his library, and there sit down among his beloved books, and pass the hours in gentle conversation with his friends, of each one of whom he seemed anxious to take a last farewell. He received them daily, in succession, during the forenoon; and towards those whom he loved particularly he showed his tenderness by kissing them when they met and when they parted. His conversation with them was of the most pleasant kind. He told them of his prospects of death, of his past life, and of his perfect calmness and reliance on God. He spoke to them of his love of moral worth. "Talents without goodness I care little for," said he to one of them. With his children he was always inexpressibly affectionate. "Come, my dears," said he, "I fear you will think me very foolish, but I cannot help telling you all how much I love you; for whenever any of you approach me, I feel as if I had a fountain of love, which gushes out upon you." He spoke to them at the dead of the night, when he awoke, pleasant as a little child, yet with the bright, clear mind of a philosopher. He told them of his life, of his desire always to be innocent, to be active in every duty, and in the acquirement of knowledge, and then alluded to a motto that he had impressed upon his mind in early life, that a good man must have a happy death. On one of these occasions he said, "I feel now quiet and happy, and I think my life has been somewhat blameless."

It was noon, and all was quiet in his library. A bright ray of light streamed through the

half-closed shutter. He was calm and free
from pain. One of his children bade him
good by for a time. Stretching out his hand
and pointing to the sunlight, he said, " Good
by, my son; the work is done; and if I knew
I were to be gone when the sun sets in the
west, I would say, ' Thy will, O God, be
done.' " Observing some around him weeping, while he was quiet, he quoted his favorite
passage from Hafiz, one of the sweetest of the
poets of Persia : —

> " So live, that, sinking in thy last long sleep,
>   Calm thou mayst smile while all around thee weep."

On another occasion, when one who was
near him had a sad countenance, he told her to
be cheerful; and then, taking Bryant's Poems
he read the four last verses of that exquisite
little poem called " The Old Man's Funeral."
It is so beautiful in itself, that I want you to
read it; and perhaps you may like to see how
he thought it applied to his own condition. I
have placed in parentheses his remarks.

THE OLD MAN'S FUNERAL.

I saw an aged man upon his bier;
   His hair was thin and white, and on his brow
A record of the cares of many a year —
   Cares that were ended and forgotten now.
And there was sadness round, and faces bowed,
And women's tears fell fast, and children wailed aloud.

Then rose another hoary man, and said,
   In faltering accents, to that weeping train,
" Why mourn ye that our aged friend is dead?
   Ye are not sad to see the gathered grain,
Nor when their mellow fruit the orchards cast,
Nor when the yellow woods shake down the ripened mast.

" Ye sigh not when the sun, his course fulfilled,
   His glorious course, rejoicing earth and sky,
In the soft evening, when the winds are stilled,
   Sinks where his islands of refreshment lie,
And leaves the smile of his departure spread
O'er the warm-colored heaven and ruddy mountain head.

" Why weep ye then for him, who, having won
   The bound of man's appointed years, at last,
Life's blessings all enjoyed, life's labors done,
   Serenely to his final rest has passed?
       [I cannot agree to the next two lines.]
While the soft memory of his virtues yet
Lingers like twilight hues when the bright sun is set.

"His youth was innocent, [yes, I believe mine was inno-
    cent; not guilty, certainly,] his riper age
Marked with some act of goodness every day, [no, not
    every day — sometimes,]
And watched by eyes that loved him, calm and sage, [O,
    yes, watched by eyes that loved him; and O, how
    calm, but I cannot add sage,]
Faded his late declining years away.
Cheerful he gave his being up, and went
To share [he hopes] the holy rest that waits a life [he hopes]
    well spent.

"That life was happy; every day he gave
    Thanks for the fair existence that was his; [yes, every
        morning, when I awoke and saw the beautiful sun
        rise, I thanked God that he had placed me in this
        beautiful world,]
For a sick fancy made him not her slave,
    To mock him with her phantom miseries.
No chronic tortures racked his aged limb,
For luxury and sloth had nourished none for him. [Yes,
    that is all true.]

"And I am glad that he has lived thus long,
    And glad that he has gone to his reward;
Nor deem that kindly nature did him wrong,
    Softly to disengage the vital cord, [O, how softly, how
        sweetly, is the cord disengaging!]
When his weak hand grew palsied, and his eye
Dark with the mists of age, it was his time to die." [Yes,
        it was his time to die; remember this; do not look
        sad or mournful; it is his time to die.]

One of the pleasant effects of his illness was his new love for flowers. He had never shown any great pleasure in them during life, although a rose, or lily of the valley, was frequently in his vest during the summer. One day during his illness, Miss —— sent him a nosegay, in the centre of which was a white camellia japonica. " Ah ! how beautiful ! " he exclaimed ; " tell her how much I am pleased ; place them where I can see them. Tell her that the japonica is to me the emblem of her spotless heart." Music, too, as it had been his delight in early life, now served to soothe his last hours. One evening, when surrounded by his family, and he was free from all pain, the door of the library was suddenly opened, and his favorite tune of Robin Adair was heard coming from some musical glasses in the entry. Its plaintiveness was always delightful to him ; and after listening to it till it died away, he exclaimed, " O, how beautiful ! I feel as if I should like to have the tune that I have loved in life prove my funeral dirge."

It was on the 15th of March, 1838, that, being too feeble to walk, he was drawn for the last time into the library. On the next day he was confined to the bed. On that day an incident took place which I cannot forbear to mention. He had called his daughter his Jessamine, and about twenty-four hours before his death she obtained for him that delicate white flower. He took it and kissed it many times. He then returned it with these words: "Take it, my love; it is beautiful; it is the queen of flowers. Let it be for you, forever, the emblem of truth and of purity. Let it be the Bowditch arms. Place it in your mother's Bible, and by the side of La Place's bust, and to-morrow, if I am alive, I will see it."

In the evening he drew a little water into his parched mouth. "How delicious!" he murmured. "I have swallowed a drop from

> ' Siloa's brook, that flowed
> Fast by the oracle of God.' "

On the morrow, 17th of March, 1838, he died. Had he lived nine days more, he would have exactly completed his sixty-fifth year. On the next Sabbath he was laid quietly by the side of his wife Mary. Snow-flakes fell gently upon the coffin as it was carried into Trinity Church vaults.

There both the bodies remained until a few years since, when they were removed to Mount Auburn.